Praise

The Deliverance is a captivating story of intrigues and manipulations.

When one person seeks to control other people's lives, it is witchcraft.

The men caught in this conniving web of bewitchment left their wives defenceless, powerless and voiceless.

The women trapped in the turmoil of the family's unresolved issues bore the trauma of depression and pregnancy loss in silence.

Until one woman stood her ground and sought deliverance on her knees because she found her voice and faith again, she fought to disentangle the web of deception and manipulations. In doing so, she brought freedom to the next generation.

Yemisi did a fantastic work with this novel as she wove the intrigues, twists and turns in the life of a woman in pursuit of love and her dreams which blinded her to the red flags in plain sight and deafened her ears to the caution from family and friends.

With this novel, Yemisi sends a note of caution to all intending to get married—don't ignore the warning signs. You will be putting your life and sanity on the line if you do.

Dr Irene T. Olumese, PhD
Inspirational Speaker and Author
Faith-Informed Transformative and Trauma Coach
Inspiring Hope, Enriching Lives

Warning alert!

The Deliverance is too captivating! I couldn't put this book down once I started. You might want to schedule a time to read this book and pen down the lessons for implementation. Prepare for a mindset cleansing. For one, ignore red flags at a cost.

A great read for spinsters and bachelors who someday want to get and stay married.

Yemisi, this one is deep! Well done!

Onyii Ejiofor
(Brand & Business Strategist)
CEO, The Atiyah Beauty Company, Brandtrybe.
IG: @heyonyii, @thatbrandchic

The Deliverance

a novel

YEMISI JOSEPH-OLOYEDE

ZAYZEE

The Deliverance

Copyright © 2022, Yemisi Joseph-Oloyede

All rights reserved. No part of this publication may be reproduced, stored in a retrieval system or transmitted in any form or by any means, electronic, mechanical, recording or otherwise (except brief passages for purposes of review) without the prior permission of the author.

ISBN: 978-978-997-853-3

Published by:

Zayzee Limited

South Pointe Estate, Off Orchid Hotel Road, Lekki, Lagos, Nigeria.

+234 8120259068

zayzeeblog@gmail.com

www.zayzeewrites.com

This is a work of fiction. Any similarities to names, events and places are purely coincidental.

Dedication

For Susan and Royalty,

You both make life worth working up to. You're strong yet tender. You're wise and learning.

I'm amazed by your sensitivity to people and things.

I'm so proud of you and love you forever.

In Marriage, two become one. Satan works to divide the one back into two. Fight for unity and peace in your marriage and honour God as a result!

— BuildYourMarriage.org

Chapter One

On a very hectic day eight years ago, Samson was standing at the bus stop waiting for a bus after attending yet another interview. He was weary and had stopped believing the promises to be in touch by the interviewers. He kept attending interviews out of routine and expecting the same outcome. Nothing.

After what seemed like an eternity, a bus heading towards Oshodi finally pulled up and he got on it thankful to be among the very few in the crowd that was heading in that direction. He had no strength left in him to struggle for any bus.

"Hold your N200 change," the conductor advised as the bus pulled out of the bus stop.

Samson's mouth fell open. He had calculated his transportation before leaving home and was already short of N50. If he paid N200, then he would be short N100 and wouldn't be able to get home.

He knew asking the bus to stop for him to get off would cause the conductor to rain curses on him. And what was the probability that he would get another bus soon, considering how long he waited?

Swallowing hard, he handed the N200 note to the conductor, committed his fate into God's hands and closed his eyes for a while to rest. He wished he could afford Gala and Coke like most of the other passengers.

Something hit his shoe and he opened his eyes. It was the lady beside him. She dropped her phone. Samson retrieved it for her.

"Thank you very much."

He nodded and turned to look outside the window.

Samson had N100 left in his wallet which would take him to Mile Two. He didn't know how he would get to Ijegun, in Satellite Town, so he stood out of people's way, looking at the faces of each conductor calling Mile Two, to judge if he could approach any and beg for a free ride. But it was rush hour.

"Hello, sir."

A lady stopped by him.

"Please help me with transport," she pleaded desperately and pointed behind her. "Can you believe somebody snatched my bag and ran across the road?" she was close to tears. Then she held out her hand with N100 in it. "This is the change the conductor gave me that I was holding. I'm going to Okoko, please sir, help me."

Samson looked at her, looked at her money and without meaning to, started laughing.

Confused, the lady stepped back and was about to walk away when Samson touched her by the arm.

"I am sorry," he said. "Sorry you got robbed. I was laughing at the coincidence because I am also thinking of how to get home. I have N100 as well."

"Oh," she was disappointed.

Samson could see how affected she was by what happened to her. "Mile Two to Okoko is N100. How will you get home from Okoko if you find N100?"

"I will take a bike and pay when I get to my sister's place."

He fished out his wallet and brought out the loan bill.

She looked at him and shook her head.

"At least one of us should get home," he tried to convince her. "I will sort myself."

She still hesitated. "What way are you going?"

"Same with you, but I will get off at Abule-Ado bus stop."

For a while, she said nothing and didn't collect the money. "Can we lap?" she surprised him.

Before he could find the right words to refuse, she had approached a conductor and beckoned to him to come quickly. "He said we should lap at the back."

It was an uncomfortable quiet ride to Mile Two with a girl sitting on his laps. When they got off the bus, she asked if she could use his phone to call her sister to tell a neighbour to pay for her bike in case her sister wasn't back from work.

"Thank you," she handed the phone back and they walked to where they would get Okoko bus for N100.

At his bus stop, they said goodbye and he got off and settled for a long walk home.

Chapter Two

Their meeting was funny. She liked to tell anyone who cared to listen that it was divine intervention that brought them together. Carefully orchestrated plans of God. One of the reasons why she stayed that long in the marriage that threatened to kill her. Despite everything, she still believed that God's words and plans never fail.

When she got home that day and narrated everything that happened to her sister, she couldn't stop laughing. The incident with Samson overshadowed the event of her being robbed. What made it quite unbelievable was the fact that she was the one who suggested that they lapped themselves in a bus.

She was very timid back then. She couldn't begin a conversation with a stranger; especially a guy.

"Is his house close to the bus stop?" Her sister, Ugochi, asked her but she didn't understand her question. "You both spent your N100 lapping each other. How did he get home from his bus stop?"

Her mouth hung open as she realised she didn't ask how he was going to get home from the bus stop.

"Chika!" Ugochi queried. "I raised you better," she joked and threw her phone at Chika. "You better call him and find out."

She was about to say she didn't collect his phone number when she realised she used his phone to call her sister so his number was on her call list.

It rang twice before she heard his voice. "Hey hi," she started. "It's the lady from Oshodi that you helped."

"Oh hello. Hope you got home safe."

"Yes, I did. I am calling to thank you and apologise as well for being inconsiderate. I didn't ask how you would get home from the bus stop."

Samson waved it away as nothing. He said she was too distressed to have been thinking of anything else. "Oh, but I walked home anyway," then he laughed. "It was good exercise."

"My name is Chika," she said and saw the look on her sister's face. They hadn't introduced themselves.

After she hung up, Ugochi, her immediate older sister, began to build castles in the air. Chika couldn't blame her. She was twenty-seven and had never had a serious relationship. Growing up among four sisters and one brother, she was the introvert in their household. Her routine was home to school and back home. She had some friends at school that she spoke to of course, but she wasn't the type to visit.

She and Ugochi went to the same university. Chika actually chose to go there because Ugochi was there. Ugochi had always been her backbone since they were children and if Chika was ever found in a crowd, Ugochi was close by.

Ugochi was two years older but preferred to play the role of mother to her little sister. And Chika always listened to her – except for one time and it almost ruined their relationship.

Chika was once set in her ways. Once she made up her mind about something, nothing and no one could make her change it. If she didn't want something, no one could make her like it. Neither their parents nor the other siblings could make her change her mind. Only Ugochi could. She was everybody's go-to person to convince Chika to do what she didn't want to do.

At school, Ugochi hooked her up three times with different guys. None of them lasted beyond two months. "He is too forward," Chika would later complain about the guy her sister introduced her to after deciding she didn't want to see the 'boyfriend material' anymore."

"What does that mean?"

She would shrug and say nothing.

"Chika, do you want to be a spinster till you die?" Ugochi asked after the third time. Chika had told her she didn't want any more introductions.

"Of course not. I don't want to be distracted. Besides, I want to get married as a virgin."

Ugochi couldn't dare complain about her reasons because that's how they were raised and Chika puts pleasing God before man.

She came to Lagos to live with Ugochi after her youth service. Ugochi had a job with a big manufacturing company based at Agbara, Ogun state, which wasn't very far from her place of residence.

Fortunately for Chika, she didn't have to job hunt for long. Within six months, she got a job as a secretary/personal assistant and her office was at Gbagada.

Chika had been in Lagos for two years when she crossed paths with Samson that day at Oshodi. She didn't know she was going to see him again, despite Ugochi's dreams of her meeting her prince charming. Chika told her the romance novels she read were clogging her thinking.

Their parents and siblings were concerned about Chika not dating. Her three other sisters before Ugochi got married before turning 27. Her only brother, the one before Ugochi was also married. Ugochi wasn't married because she refused to. Her longtime boyfriend asked her and she told him they should wait till he returned to the country because he was going to do his Master's in the UK.

"I am not going to be a single married woman," she told Chika.

They all thought she was making a mistake but Ugochi insisted she would prefer to lose the boyfriend than lose a husband. Ike obviously, wasn't going to lose her. He kept in touch with her and with their parents too. His parents also communicated regularly with the in-laws so, in a way, both families knew they were waiting for Ike to return and Ugochi would be married.

Other than not having a boyfriend, Chika felt her life was perfect. She was single and doing life God's way. She had a dream of a future she was aspiring to.

Being a 27-year-old virgin who had only kissed one person wasn't a big deal. Her future was in view, marriage and having kids were on her mind. She was waiting for the right guy to come along. She didn't believe she had to kiss every frog to find her prince.

Also, her relationship with God was better than ever, and, she believed God was taking her somewhere special.

Destiny is no matter of chance. It is a matter of choice. It is not a thing to be waited for, it is a thing to be achieved.

— William Jennings Bryan

Chapter Three

After that first meeting, Samson caught himself occasionally thinking about Chika and wondered what she would think if he called her just to check on her. Apart from the time she called to confirm he got home, she didn't call again. He also knew he would have to call her sister to speak with her since she lost her phone in her bag, and he didn't know if she had retrieved her line. That discouraged him.

Besides, he reminded himself that his priority was getting a job. He felt at that point in his life, he didn't have anything to offer anyone. He had baggage he was yet to deal with and no idea how to go about it.

His friend Maro, whom he lived with, kept reassuring him that everything would work out, and Samson tried to take his advice. While he didn't give up on finding a job, he continued the private tutoring of three teenagers on the street who were preparing for WAEC.

The N30,000 he got monthly from them gave him a little something to hold for his transportation around town and to buy a few things in the house even though Maro told him not to bother.

He met Maro at the university and they became good friends. Maro had been posted to serve in Lagos and the telecommunications company where he served retained his services.

Maro was the one he called when he fell out of favour with his father. Samson had not been asked to leave home or resign his position at his father's company where he worked as an Operations Manager at Safe Travels since he left school. He felt it was the right thing to do at the time to step back and understand what he wanted to do with his life.

His father started Safe Travels, an inter-country transportable company with a single bus when Samson was 11 years old. By the time he graduated from the university at 23, Safe Travels was one of the most reliable transportation companies in the country, with branches in more than 20 states.

His elder brother was the general manager and his elder sister headed finance and administration. They all grew up understanding they would work at the company. His father made them all study courses in line with the area he wanted each child to work in the company. Samson always desired something else but didn't mention it anymore after the first time he attempted.

When he left his father, he thought he would work on his dreams and prove to his family that he could be successful at it, but things hadn't gone the way he planned.

His mum called him occasionally to check on him and convince him to apologise to his father and return home. He knew if he needed to change his employment status, he would have to swallow his pride and go to his father.

That was looking to be like his only option, more so because he couldn't live with Maro forever. His friend was getting married soon and would move to a new place. Samson could only remain where he was until the rent expired. After that, he had no idea what his next steps would be.

One Saturday, he and Maro went to the beach for a hangout organised by the church's media department. Every member was permitted to invite a friend. Their contribution towards the hangout provided for that. Maro brought his fiancée and while Samson didn't invite anyone, he joked that he just might find an impromptu guest at the beach to invite.

They had a great time with Samson acting as the photographer for the event. He left the others for a while to walk along the shoreline, thinking how absurd it would be to run into any of his family members because that was the beach they frequented; especially his sister.

He shrugged off the thought as he played with his phone, taking pictures of his legs when the waves hit them.

"Hello?"

Samson looked up. She was smiling at him. He smiled back at the stranger who crawled up to him without him noticing.

"I saw you earlier but I wasn't sure you were the one," she said. "I had to come to ask, maybe I'm mistaken. Samson?" she asked, he nodded and she threw herself at him as she hugged him.

Samson lost his balance and they fell. In that split second, he flung his phone.

"Oh my God, I am so sorry," she apologised as they struggled to their feet. "I am sorry." She was embarrassed.

"It's okay," he said looking around for his phone. "I dropped my phone," he said.

"Oh," she started to look around as well. "There," she pointed happily as she raced to fetch it. It was on dry sand.

"Thank you," he collected the phone and looked at her without recognition.

THE DELIVERANCE

She smiled shyly. "You don't recognise me," she stated. "Chika. We met at …"

"Yes," he smiled. "I was just about to say that."

Chika smiled in relief. "You are the last person I expected to run into here. And to think I didn't want to come."

They laughed.

"Samson!"

Maro was waving him over.

He took her by the hand. "Come."

They walked together in silence towards his group.

"Oya now? Closing prayer, so whoever wants to leave can leave," the group leader said. "And Samson finally brought his guest. Friend of Samson, welcome. Welfare, please attend to our guest."

Samson introduced her as his friend he had just run into at the beach.

"Hey Chika, I didn't know Samson had a beautiful girlfriend like you."

"Eh, no em …" she stammered.

"Don't mind him," Samson told her to relax. "He's just being nosy. This is my very good friend, Maro…"

Some minutes later, they all left together in Maro's car. Samson sat at the back with Chika and her sister. They dropped off Itunu, Maro's girlfriend, first, before Chika and Ugochi got off at Abule-Ado to join a bus to their final destination.

"Damn. I forgot to collect her number," Samson realised. "I have her sister's number though."

Maro wagged a finger at him. "You have been keeping this secret from me."

Samson laughed and told him how they met. "So, it's nothing."

"By chance meeting two times," Maro nodded. "She seems like a nice person. If I were you …" he smiled and kept quiet.

That night, Chika called to thank him for the ride.

"You still have my number?" he was surprised.

"Well, I actually copied it from my sister's phone that day and have had it since I retrieved my line."

That made him glad. "I also kept your sister's number too and sometimes thought of calling you."

They were quiet.

"So, why didn't you call?" she asked.

He hesitated. "I wasn't sure how you would have felt."

"I would have liked it."

Samson smiled. "Now that I have your number, I will call you."

They spoke for another thirty minutes.

I know God has a plan. I pray for direction to follow it, patience to wait on it, and knowledge to know when it comes.

— GodFruits.com

Chapter Four

After meeting Samson that first time, his phone number was the first Chika saved after she got another phone and retrieved her line. She thought about him more than a few times. She didn't know him well enough but felt he was a good person. She also felt they could be good friends but because she had never been an initiator of any kind of friendship, she didn't dare call him. She wished he would call her instead.

When a month went by and he didn't, she shrugged it off and believed he must have forgotten the stranded girl he met. She had been surprised and happy to see him at the beach she didn't want to go to, but Ugochi insisted because she just wanted to hang out.

Chika had noticed the group when she and her sister walked past them as they were dancing. Then she saw him with his phone taking pictures of the dancers. "That guy looks familiar," she told her sister. "But I don't know where I know him from."

"The only guy who's probably in your memory is the one who lapped you in a bus," Ugochi said. She never stopped teasing Chika about it. But, she was correct, it was him. Chika stopped as she looked at him again.

"Go and say hello," Ugochi pushed.

"No way," Chika responded. Later, Ugochi pointed out that he was alone, and urged Chika to go say hello.

Chika hesitated. "What if he is not the one?"

Ugochi raised both hands. "Then you apologise. It's not a big deal, Chika."

She was right again.

"Have you called him to thank him and his friend?" Ugochi started later that night. Chika had it in mind but didn't want to be too forward especially when he didn't ask for her number.

"He didn't ask for my number."

Her sister looked at her silently, shook her head and walked away. She knew Chika had his number. Chika was still battling with the decision to call or not to call when Ugochi returned, picked up her phone and dialled his number. She put it on speaker and dropped it by Chika's side.

THE DELIVERANCE

"Didn't you notice how pleased he was to see you and talk with you?" Ugochi asked.

"Hello?" Samson answered the phone and Ugochi walked away.

They spoke for a little over 30 minutes about several things, and she got to know about his job hunting and accommodation situation.

The following week, she called to invite him to a training her office was organizing on entrepreneurship and Samson thoroughly enjoyed it. It was when he asked the facilitator a question that she realised he was interested in photography. After the training had ended, he waited an extra hour for her to close and they went home together.

He told her of his plans to get a job and work for a year or two. He also mentioned that he wanted to gather funds to start his photography business. The training had opened his eyes to see that he could start with his phone as it had a good camera. What was left was for him to make a plan.

Chika also shared her dreams with him. Apparently, she loved fashion and making good clothes, and it dawned on her that she could improve on her basic knowledge, so, she was saving to go to a fashion school.

With her basic knowledge, she made simple styles for herself, family members and some neighbours, when she had the time. Besides, she was also working to ensure she had enough money saved for pocket money till her sewing business would stabilize. Going to fashion school for a year meant leaving her current job and Chika didn't want to depend on anyone. All her siblings had their own families and Ugochi was getting married in a matter of months, so Chika would have to pay her own rent.

"That's so good," he told her.

After a while, she realised she liked him a lot but she didn't want to agree that she had fallen in love with him. But she could tell herself she liked him a lot. He was different from the few guys she allowed herself to get close to in the past. He wasn't very forward, he didn't cross any boundaries in their conversations, and he was extremely respectful.

Chika felt very comfortable around him and didn't have to put up any guard. He would ask a question and keep quiet to listen. He loved to listen to her talk. The only things she had to talk about were her work and her faith in God.

"Do you have friends?" he asked one day. He had come over to Ugochi's place to visit her and watched as she made an Ankara top.

Chika didn't have close friends. She always hung around Ugochi so she considers most of her sister's friends her friends. She just didn't have that close friendship with anybody else that she could gossip with. At that time though, some of her colleagues had become her friends.

Not that they had to gossip about anything. Chika was very private and never allowed people to know her thoughts or plans; not even Ugochi, though her sister could guess.

"What about you?" She asked him.

"Maro is my closest friend," he said. "We met at school and he's been God sent." He fell quiet before continuing. "He took me in when I stopped working at Safe Travels and had nowhere to go."

"You worked at Safe Travels?"

He smiled and nodded.

"The same Safe Travels I enter to the East to see my parents?" Chika wanted to be sure.

Samson nodded. "I was the Operations Manager for five years. Just until a couple of months ago when I resigned."

"Oh wow."

"That's in the past now," he smiled and picked up his phone to busy himself taking pictures of her at work.

How come he worked for five years and didn't try to invest anything into his dream? She wondered but didn't ask.

That should have been the first sign for her back then, but she didn't grasp it. She was just lost in the moment of having this friend who fitted everything she wanted in a man, even though she never made a list.

When she mentioned to her sister later that Samson worked for five years as an Operations Manager at Safe Travels, she was surprised and asked the same question Chika wondered about.

"How old is he?" she asked Chika.

"28."

"So, he started working there when he was 23. He is not married, he doesn't have children, he doesn't have a car, and immediately he stopped working, he moved in with his friend. What was he doing with his money?"

Chika had no idea. "Maybe he has family responsibilities."

Ugochi made a face. "Maybe. But find out. What has he told you about his family?"

Chika shook her head.

"Hmmm. Chika, learn to ask questions okay? Let him tell you about his family then you will know if it was family responsibility that's responsible for him not having any form of saving. Some people can lack character and discipline where money is concerned. You don't want to end up with such a person."

"We are just friends, Ugochi," Chika reminded her even though deep down, she was building monstrous castles. "And besides, it will look as if I am prying."

Ugochi gave her an incredible look. "Won't you become friends first before you end up with someone?" she asked Chika. "And won't you know who a person is before you decide to become friends with him? In case you don't know, where a person is from, how he was raised, and everything he inherited from his parents contributes to who a person is. That includes the parents' character and so on. And before you tell me I am jumping the gun, don't deny it. I see how your face lights up when you talk about him and I am happy. But the fact that I want my sister to at least date someone doesn't mean it has to be the first guy who comes along and has already given us a questionable picture into his pocket management. Pocket management is very important. You know Aunty Nkechi's story. Let it guide you o."

Ugochi was right but Chika was sure there was a good explanation for that because Samson seemed to be just perfect. He was also God-fearing and committed to service in God's house. Why wouldn't a girl like Chika put that first above all else? It was like hitting the jackpot. God gave her the perfect gift in reward for living a life of purity.

She had this deep conviction that God's hands were involved in their meeting and she was certain whatever the negatives that came up, they wouldn't stand up to the plenty positives she saw in him.

She could see her dreams falling into place one after the other. Her fashion design business and her marriage and raising a godly family. What she wanted fitted into the context of what marriage should be; to join herself and become one with a man, to submit in marriage to him, acknowledge him as the head of the home as the Bible teaches and most importantly, to do purpose together.

She believed she was on that track. She knew where Samson was heading because he shared his dreams with her. She shared hers too. They were already good support for each other and were going to cheer one another on to achieve their personal dreams and the ones they will set for their family, if indeed God had brought them together to be one, which she already believed was the case.

She always believed wholesome is key! But somewhere along the line, the perfect picture of them—the dream and all the purposes—got hit and her life began to spiral out of control.

It was unbelievable.

Getting hit is an understatement. What she entered shook her, destabilised her and dumped her in a pit of depression. Round and round she went, trying to climb out, but lower and deeper she sank.

She was warned. She saw the red flags. She disregarded them all because she felt she knew the way to stir the wheel.

THE DELIVERANCE

It took her years of pain to finally understand that submission in marriage does not come at the expense of one's peace of mind.

Those days that she sat and cried, she asked herself why. She and Ugochi saw the signs and her sister advised her rightly. She couldn't understand how she allowed herself to be manipulated and controlled to the extent that she lost her voice and had no say in her home. She almost lost her dreams as well.

Initially, Chika was full of regrets which progressed into self-loathing because she blamed herself for where she was. She was a complete mental wreck and got to a stage where she decided that life would be a much better place for others without her in it. She picked up a knife to save herself from herself. She had had enough.

To have peace and love in a marriage is a gift that is next to the knowledge of the gospel.

— Martin Luther

Chapter Five

Chika was drunk in love. Although Samson had never asked her out and they had never spoken about having a relationship, it just happened that they spoke to each other first thing in the morning and the last thing before they slept.

She knew his lack of employment worried him but she made sure to encourage him. He wanted to have a weekday job, while he dedicated weekends to his photography. He attached himself to a photographer to learn a few more tricks that were good for him.

When Maro was preparing for his wedding, he asked Samson to cover it. This was Samson's first big coverage and he was excited! There was an initial tussle between him and Maro over the coverage because Maro wanted to pay the average industry standard but Samson was bent on doing the job pro bono.

Maro knew he couldn't change Samson's mind so he did the next best thing he could think of. Because they had talked about it before, he knew the type of camera Samson wanted so he bought it and some other needed equipment. That way Samson didn't have to borrow a camera to cover the wedding.

Samson had been emotional and promised he was going to pay back.

"It's a gift and an investment into your future," Maro told him. "It is not a loan."

Chika and her sister attended Maro's wedding together and when Ugochi saw the pictures, she also asked Samson to cover her wedding which was two months after Maro's.

Samson asked her not to pay anything and Ugochi laughed and looked at her sister. "Samson, I think you need to go take a course on how to run a business. Seriously. How will you transport yourself to Enugu for the wedding? How would you pay for a hotel?"

Samson hesitated. "I actually didn't think of that."

"My sister is very good with money. She can teach you a few things," Ugochi smiled at him.

Chika knew Ugochi paved the way for her to ask Samson the big question about his money management skill. A month after he told her about his past employment, she still hadn't found the perfect time to ask him.

THE DELIVERANCE

When Ugochi left them, Chika asked if he was going to continue paying the rent for the two-bedroom apartment. Maro had moved to Surulere with his wife.

"I haven't decided," Samson told her. "The rent expires in four months."

"Can you afford it or do you need to move to a smaller place?"

"If I can get events to cover every weekend, I will be able to afford it."

Chika didn't like his answer. "Samson, you cannot plan based on the money you do not have."

He smiled. "Don't worry your pretty head. I have good money management skills. Don't forget I worked …"

"At Safe Travels for five years as the Operations Manager," she interrupted him.

He smiled and nodded.

The moment of truth finally arrived.

"Babe?" she started. "Can I ask you something?"

He nodded.

"Was it a good job at Safe Travels? Did it pay well?"

He nodded.

"Why didn't you start your photography since? You could have been able to afford a camera earlier if you had saved right?"

"Of course."

"So why didn't you? Don't be angry. I'm just curious why you had to move in with Maro after you resigned."

Samson was quiet for a while and she thought he wasn't going to answer her. He kept on flipping through the TV stations. "It's a long and unhappy story," he looked at her.

Chika saw the cloud that suddenly took over his expression. "Do you want to tell me?"

He sighed, dropped the remote control and faced her. "I knew this day was going to come so we might as well get it over with, then you can decide if I'm worth your time."

She said nothing.

"I studied Business Administration because that was what my dad wanted. I managed to graduate. I didn't like it. It wasn't what I wanted to do. I and my siblings all had our courses chosen for us."

He told the family once about his dreams but his father talked it down because he didn't understand the type of photography Samson wanted. Samson knew his father was only looking out to secure the future of his children but Samson had been very unhappy at the job. Then one day he decided to follow his dreams and he resigned immediately before he could lose his courage.

Chika listened to him attentively.

"I knew it was going to cause some conflicts which I avoided by moving out immediately. I planned to pursue this dream and prove to my family that I could be successful at it. And you met me looking for a job to fund my dream."

She nodded. "Okay. So, you were living at home with your folks. Did you have savings?"

Samson rubbed his face. "No, I did not because I was not on salary."

Chika frowned. "You were not on salary for five years as a manager? How?"

He shrugged. "I had access to one of the company's accounts. We all did. The company has different bank accounts. I and my siblings are signatories to at least one account each that we could take care of our needs from. They were more like our personal accounts, but they were in the company's name."

Chika was lost. "Your siblings were also working at Safe Travels?"

He gave her a funny look. "Yes. That's what I'm saying. My dad carefully planned our lives to secure our future.

My elder brother is the general manager, my sister heads the finance and admin, I was heading operations and my younger brother heads logistics."

Chika was quiet.

"Oh, I'm sorry. You don't understand. My dad owns Safe Travels. It's our family business."

Chika opened her mouth. "Wow." She finally understood.

"So, I have baggage," he said and smiled.

Chika suddenly pitied him. She cherished family. She grew up in a tight-knit family. She couldn't imagine having a conflict with her parents. She wouldn't even dare. Her eldest sister, Adaeze would chop her to pieces before she tried. But she knew there could never be a reason for her to be in any kind of conflict with her parents because they were brought up to speak their minds and have an opinion about their lives.

They weren't half as wealthy as Samson's family but her parents gave them good education which they believed was enough for them to work with to secure their future.

"Are you in contact with anyone in your family?" she asked him.

He sighed. "My mum calls occasionally. She wants me to come back home."

THE DELIVERANCE

She reached for his hand. "I'm so sorry. That must be a burden to carry."

Chika wasn't going to say anything about Samson, but when they all gathered in their hometown for Ugochi's wedding, her sister made sure to tell their parents and siblings that Samson and Chika had been together for seven months.

Everybody drilled Chika. Where was he from? What are his family people like? Had she met them? Are they receptive? So many questions that Chika could not answer.

"What do you mean you haven't met anyone in his family and you've been together for seven months?" her eldest sister, Adaeze, asked.

Chika had no choice but to tell them what she knew.

"Chika," Nonso, her brother called her attention. "Think carefully dear. I don't doubt that he is a good person. I've been engaging him since he arrived and I like him, but you cannot put aside the family."

She knew that. Chika had been worried since Samson told her about his family. She didn't know how it was going to affect them.

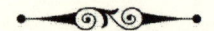

One thing I learned a long time ago was to never ignore the red flags in the beginning, or they'll be the same reason it all ends.

— M. Sosa

Chapter Six

The Omoefe family were delighted to welcome them. Chika was surprised. She thought the occasion was going to be tense considering how Samson left his job and his family, but his father was full of smiles when he hugged him. His mum and siblings were all so happy it felt more like Samson went on a trip and had just returned.

Chika was warmly received as Samson's girlfriend. Samson's father even thanked her for being the reason why his son finally came home. They were all genuinely happy that Chika immediately felt drawn to them.

There were lots of talks, but it was mostly Chika who was answering questions that were thrown at her.

While they ate lunch, Samuel, the elder brother asked Samson what he's been up to.

"Where do you work now?"

For a few seconds, the table fell quiet and Chika saw Samson's unease.

"I do photography," Samson said.

Silence.

"You once said you wanted to do that thing," his father remarked and said nothing more.

"Chika my daughter," his mother changed the subject. "How early do you leave home if your office is at Gbagada and you live at Okoko? Is the traffic situation on that road better now?"

"It's actually getting worse," Chika admitted. "But I leave home at 5:00 a.m. and before 8:00 a.m. I'm in the office."

"That must be a lot of stress," Stella, Samson's only sister said.

Chika nodded. "I'm moving once my rent expires. The location was convenient for my sister because it was close to her job, but she is in Abuja now with her husband."

They continued the rest of their lunch in silence, with occasional small talks that had nothing to do with Chika or Samson.

When it came time for them to leave, Mrs. Funke Omoefe was disappointed they weren't spending the night. Chika apologised and said she hadn't prepared for that, and she had to go to work the next day.

THE DELIVERANCE

"Okay," Mr. Omoefe cleared his throat. "Samson, before you leave, I have to say something."

Samson nodded as if he's been expecting it.

"You didn't have to leave the way you did. Your mother was very sad," he paused to look at his wife who nodded at him. "Especially because you had no money on you other than …" he looked to Stella for help.

"He withdrew N30,000 a week before," she provided.

"Right. You had no money on you. You left your car and most of your things. I'm not going to ask you why, but you should know you worked very hard and didn't deserve to leave the way you did empty handed. Your mother and I started this business to make everybody's future secure whether or not you are under this roof. You are all part owners of Safe Travels. So, go with your car, please. Solomon, give him his keys."

The youngest son handed over the keys to Samson. "Thank you, sir," Samson said.

"I want to see you more okay?" his father told him when they were outside. "Chika, don't let him run away again from his family, please."

Chika smiled.

They were quiet as they drove away from Ikoyi in Samson's Toyota Camry. Chika allowed him to process his thoughts.

"What do you think?" he asked suddenly. They had driven past Oshodi. "My family."

Chika shrugged. "I don't know. They all appeared really pleased to see you."

"And?"

"And I was surprised," she admitted. "Considering what you told me, I was expecting ... I don't know what I was expecting honestly. But I didn't expect such warm reception. There was no tension; you were the only tensed one as if you were expecting something to happen."

"No," he said. "We are a loving family. We all just have to do things my dad's way that's all."

Chika said nothing. The man didn't seem that way to her but what did she know? "Do all your siblings live at home?"

"Except Samuel. He's married. He lives in Lekki Phase 1."

Chika smiled. "I noticed all your names begin with 'S'."

He nodded. "My dad is Simon, but mum is Funke."

"She's Yoruba?"

He nodded. "Please open the glove compartment."

She did.

"What's in it?"

Chika saw the car papers and two cheque books.

"I guessed as much," he said and the rest of the journey was in silence till they got to Satellite Town. Chika had agreed to spend the night there because they knew they might return late.

It was her first time sleeping over. It was the first time he asked her to and she accepted because it made more sense. Samson had been an extreme gentleman with her that at times, she actually wondered. They kissed all the time, but even in the moments she had almost gotten carried away, he stopped them.

They never spoke about it. They never talked about sex and he didn't know she wanted to remain a virgin till she was married. He didn't know she was a virgin. She concluded he had the same plans as her. He was either a virgin as well, or committed to abstinence till he was married.

They had a very light dinner and Samson hardly ate. "Are you okay?" she asked him.

"My dad didn't say anything about my photography."

Chika sighed. "Maybe you didn't try to make him understand you before."

"Maybe," he agreed. "He's going to tell me to come back to work."

Chika considered that carefully. "You are still looking for a job," she said. "The studio where you intern three times a week, does not pay you."

"I have learnt a lot," he admitted.

"I support whatever decision you make," she said, unsure of what that meant because going by that day's visit, she saw that Samson took the easy way out. He didn't fight for what he wanted. He told her he mentioned his desire to do photography just one time. She felt he should have shown them how serious he was. He was afraid of a conflict that probably wouldn't have happened.

"Babe," he interrupted her thoughts.

Chika looked up at him. He was looking straight at her. He had a strange look.

"Let's get married," he dropped. "I don't ever want to live without you by my side."

Chika didn't react immediately.

He touched her face and smiled. "Do you have any idea how much you have affected my life in the eight months we have known each other? You gave me wings to fly. You believe in my dreams too and I love you," he smiled. It was his first time using the L-word. "You help me make the right decisions because I find myself these days, thinking how whatever I do affects you and us. Can you imagine it never occurred to me I could actually attach myself to a photographer and learn to develop the skills for my dreams? I never looked into what I had to do to become a photographer. I just knew I wanted to be one and I thought the first thing I needed was a camera. But when we started communicating and the way you ask questions about my dreams, my eyes opened to so many things. True confession," he laughed. "Even Maro noticed and warned me never to lose you. And you were right, it was stupid of me not to have invested in myself all the years I was working. I had access to good money. I should have taken some photography courses online, bought some gadgets, found some ways to develop myself, but I didn't. I felt I had to stop working."

Chika felt her doubts slip off her shoulders. "I'm glad. The past, what you did or didn't do, is not important. Now and where you want to go is more important."

"Let's go there together," he winked at her. "Let's do now, do tomorrow, do forever and achieve our dreams together. Marry me, fairy godmother," he brought his face close to hers, their noses touching.

"Let's do life together," she whispered. "I'm ready."

They kissed. Passionately. She was carried away and didn't care. Samson didn't stop.

That night, they gave themselves to each other as they swore their undying love.

Chapter Seven

Everything else happened very fast. Samson's mother called her the next day while she was at work to thank her for bringing her son home. She prayed for Chika and said she would love to have Chika as a daughter-in-law. Chika was very pleased.

She called Ugochi to give her the good news and her sister was happy as well. "This Samson obviously lacks some guts I see," Ugochi said and they laughed.

Samson picked her up from work which surprised her because they didn't agree on that. He said he wanted to get her home so she could pick up some of her things and come stay the whole week with him.

"That's not right," she said when she got into the car.

"You are my wife now."

She shook her head. "Not yet."

He nodded and smiled at her silently for a few seconds. "Thank you."

She frowned. "For what?"

He smiled and kissed her quickly. "For waiting for me. For making me your first. It is the purest gift I've received in my life."

Chika looked away shyly. "I thought you didn't realise."

He sighed contently. "You are mine forever babe. Mine alone."

Mid-week, Samson told her his dad called to invite him back to work and gave him all the time he needed to decide. "I thought I needed to prove to my family that I could be successful by following my heart. But I don't think I need to prove anything to anyone. What I really wanted when I left was to find myself and understand what I needed to do to be on the right path towards fulfilling my dreams. And I think I have achieved that. So, I just have to ensure I stay on track."

She smiled.

"I will go back," he told her. "But I will resume after we are married."

She frowned. They hadn't set any dates or talked about his family going to see hers.

THE DELIVERANCE

"It will give us time to find a place on the Island. Maybe you should start thinking of resigning and going to the fashion school you talked about."

Just two weeks after she met his whole family, they all travelled to the east to see her parents. All her siblings travelled down as well. It was a peaceful introduction of families.

Later on, her family asked her why they wanted to get married so quickly when they hadn't done marriage classes at church. Chika told them they already registered at his church and the classes were for twelve weeks. They would get married immediately after.

She could see her parents and her eldest sister weren't fully as enthusiastic as the others.

"Chika, you only met his family once, apart from this visit. You haven't really spent time with them, have you?" her mother asked and she shook her head.

"Why don't you get to know them a little more?" her eldest sister asked. "They do seem like nice people, but, the more time you spend with someone, the better you know the person."

"His father is softly spoken and very suggestive. In a manipulative way, I can't explain it," her brother said.

He wasn't the only one who noticed that. It crossed Chika's mind as well.

Her parents expressed their happiness concerning their planned union but they advised her not to rush.

When she returned to Lagos, Samson's mother called to ask if she could start planning the wedding. Chika was speechless.

"I am just excited my daughter," she said. "And you know everything has to be perfect. So, we have to start planning now. And you don't have to worry my dear. I will take all the stress off you. All you have to do is look pretty and get married."

Chika didn't know whether to be happy his family loved her so much and wanted her to be one of them as soon as possible, or be worried because like her family said, they were rushing.

Samson took her to go check out an apartment in Ikoyi, and a semi-detached duplex in Lekki. He hadn't returned to work yet at Safe Travels, and other than Maro and Ugochi's weddings, he hadn't covered any other event. He didn't have money to afford any of the places they checked and she told him that.

He smiled. "We are not paying. Either the apartment or the duplex, your choice. They are both ours."

THE DELIVERANCE

Chika didn't understand. "Whose?"

"My dad's," he said. "Let's take the duplex. It has four rooms and you can turn one into your workstation."

"Your brother is just on the other side of this duplex," she noted.

He nodded. "Yes. It's good, right? Family."

Chika wasn't convinced. She didn't know why she was suddenly bothered. The enthusiasm in Samson was different.

"If you don't like it, we can take the apartment," he offered the other option.

The apartment was a few blocks from his parents' place. She didn't like it either. "Do we have to take either of these?"

"These are the empty properties we have at the moment."

She told him they could rent and it didn't have to be on the Island which they obviously could not afford.

His mother called her the next day about the properties and Chika realised Samson must have told them they weren't moving to the Island. She told Chika how she and her husband struggled in Lagos and vowed none of their children would go through what they endured.

"We just want to make things easy, so you can start your lives easy and without stress," then the woman laughed. "If I had been given such a gift when I married Simon, I would have jumped at it. Think about it, dear. How can my daughter-in-law be in a rented place when we have properties all over the place?"

Chika turned to Ugochi, who said there was nothing wrong with her in-laws wanting to give them accommodation, but she didn't like the proximity.

Samson's mother called her mother about planning the wedding and told her it would be nice to use an event centre for the engagement in Enugu, instead of doing it at their family compound. She told Chika's mother very important guests would come and they wanted everybody to be comfortable.

Her family didn't like it. They didn't know Chika and Samson still wanted to go with their initial dates which they told her was too soon.

"Chika, you're just accepting everything these people are telling you. Are you sure you want to marry this Samson? Are you part of these decisions?"

Chika was stressed and confused. She didn't know when a simple and growing relationship with Samson turned into a circus and she wasn't happy about it. Where to live, the whole marriage thing was causing tension between them. When she realised they have printed wedding invitation cards, she was very upset because Samson didn't consult her about it and they went ahead with the dates her family was yet to agree to. They picked venues for the reception she had no say in. They picked colours for her wedding.

"We haven't even done an introduction!" Chika screamed at him.

Samson apologised and said some invitations have already been sent because his mum likes to get things done immediately.

She had looked at him in silence before calmly saying she didn't believe any of the IVs had been sent out. They were just using that as a tactic to get her and her family to agree to the dates.

"Babe," he took her hand. "Don't you want to marry me anymore? I thought we both wanted this. I'm sorry about my mum, but it's who she is. You should have seen her during Samuel's wedding. She's just excited to be having another daughter," he smiled at her. "Can't you see how much you have charmed her?"

Chika's heart melted. She knew he was right. She believed there was really no point waiting longer to get married if they could earlier. She knew her family also wanted time to plan, especially the expense. She resolved within she would talk to her parents. She could take up part of her family's expenses with her savings. She just didn't want to feel as if his family were trying so hard to make her a part of them, and she was pulling back.

Even Samuel's wife was excited at the thought of having Samson and Chika live next door and their children growing up together, that Chika had to wonder why she had reservations when the whole family had been so nice and loving towards her.

But when her father called that he received some packs of invitations for their guests, he was upset because Chika had failed to update them. Everyone in her family was upset.

Samson's mother flew to Enugu with her sister to apologise and beg. She said she thought they were on the same page, and that it was a miscommunication. Most of the invitations had gone out and the event centres will charge them for cancellation. "Let's just fix a date for the introduction, so we can follow the dates on the IV for the engagement here and the wedding in Lagos."

"Chika, I have a bad feeling about all of this," Ugochi told her on the phone. "Why isn't Samson telling them your desires? Or is this what you want?"

It was what she wanted. She wanted to be married to the love of her life. And just like Samson, she didn't want any conflicts either considering how nice the Omoefe family was and she wanted her family to just go along.

THE DELIVERANCE

While speaking on the phone with Adaeze, her eldest sister, Chika offered her savings to help with some of the expenses in the little time they had to plan and her eldest sister took offence. "Are you the one giving yourself out? Can't the family do its part to marry off a daughter? Chika? I don't recognise you anymore. You went to Lagos to pursue a dream. Have you forgotten that? Of course, Samson seems nice but I do not like how you seem to just allow anything. Where is your will in all of these?"

Chika was stressed. Nobody told her preparing for marriage could trigger conflicts in families.

"I know families usually clash when preparing for a wedding and all. People say the wedding events are for the families and not the bride and groom but this one is too much. They are trying to manipulate all of us to do as they want. Chika, this is not right."

Ugochi felt terrible for encouraging her sister to be with Samson. They didn't realise that one red flag they noticed about his pocket management was deeper. Chika should have seen it was wrong for him or his siblings not to be on salaries simply because they had access to the company's accounts.

Chika was also sad. Since she graduated, her family had given different hints in words and actions to let her know they were waiting for her to get married. She knew they constantly asked Ugochi if she was in any relationship.

Chika had been a good daughter; a very responsible one and she felt the least her family could do for her was not make her confused. She and Samson were ready. It was only her family that was holding back. The lack of support hurt her and made her feel as though they weren't happy she was happy.

Chapter Eight

Her family invited her to the East for a family meeting because Samson's family had been pressuring them about doing the introduction since the engagement date was drawing close.

They wanted Chika to do the right thing and postpone the wedding. "Give yourself time to know this family better," her brother advised. "I do not understand the rush. And I do not like how they used the invitation cards to manipulate us. Can you talk to them?"

Chika knew it would be embarrassing to Samson's family because they had sent out the invitations. It wasn't really about losing a part of the deposit for the event centres booked for the receptions, it was more about the embarrassment. Since meeting his family, they've involved her in many family affairs and introduced her as Samson's fiancée. People will wonder why they had to postpone the wedding and her in-laws will not like it.

Her other fear, which she couldn't tell anyone, was falling out of favour with Samson's family. It could affect her relationship with Samson. Should that happen, she didn't know how long it would take her to meet the next right person, or if she would be able to forget Samson.

They were good together. They were in love. She had given herself to him because in her head, as far as she was concerned, they were already one. She kept herself for just one man.

"Are you blinded by all the wealth?" her mother asked her.

"No!" Chika rejected the idea. "When I met Samson, I didn't know his family and we were already together before his family came into the picture."

Everybody took turns through that weekend to convince her to hold on and not rush but Chika's mind was made up. Not even Ugochi, the only one who could make her change her mind, could do anything.

Chika saw they were all convinced she was making a mistake. She wondered why they couldn't see things from where she stood and how loving and welcoming Samson's family had been to her. She thought every family would want their daughter to marry into such a loving atmosphere instead of trying to erect walls.

She saw that the stress and confusion she'd faced since the whole marriage topic began had been caused solely by her

THE DELIVERANCE

family. Samson's elder brother had asked her if her family felt the Omoefe's weren't good enough and Chika had been embarrassed.

"Okay," her father decided finally. "Since this is what you want, we will support you. But you know how we feel about this, but we will support you and pray that all our worries will come to nothing. They will be just worries and nothing else. We want you to be happy, and if this is where your happiness lies, we will support you."

Everyone took time to advise her and wish her well, even though she could see their reluctance. Everyone except Ugochi, who said Chika should hold on.

"I cannot place my hand on it, but something is just not right," she insisted later to Chika. "You know I love you and want the best for you. I am not comfortable with how I feel about all of these. And since you told me you and Samson settled to live in the duplex, I've only felt unrest in my spirit. Chika, have you been praying about this?"

Chika nodded and told her sister she was 100% convinced about Samson.

Ugochi was quiet for a while. "Maybe Samson is the one, but I strongly believe it is not the right time to marry him."

Then Chika told her sister what she's kept to herself. She only found out two days before travelling. "I'm pregnant."

"No," Ugochi refused to believe it. "But..."

"Yes. I know. It happened and kept on," Chika said.

"This is more reason why you shouldn't get married right now," Ugochi said. "You aren't making the right decisions. You know you shouldn't get married simply because you are pregnant. And you won't tell…"

"I'm not telling anyone and neither are you, Ugo. Even Samson does not know."

Ugochi shook her head at the complication.

Back in Lagos, Ugochi kept trying to convince her sister to halt the wedding. At a point, Chika began to avoid taking her calls. Her family was finally on board. She just wanted to get married.

Her plan of not wanting anyone to know she was pregnant didn't work as she started feeling nauseous and her mother-in-law guessed correctly. The family was excited about welcoming their first grandchild as Samuel and his wife were yet to have a child.

It was Samson's mother who broke the news to her mother and Chika once again had to convince her parents she was doing the right thing, and she didn't know about the pregnancy either.

If anything, the news of her pregnancy increased the doubts her family already had. But nobody tried to stop her anymore. The introduction came and went, the engagement and the wedding also came and went.

They were all beautiful occasions and everyone was happy, including her family.

By the time they got married, she was already eight weeks into her first trimester.

She and Samson finally moved into the duplex that was beautifully furnished by Samuel and his wife, their wedding gifts to her and Samson. Samson's parents also gave them a car.

They settled into married life. Chika had stopped working a month before they got married because she and Samson agreed she should go on the fashion course immediately after they were married.

But because of her pregnancy, her mother-in-law advised her to put that plan on hold, being that it was her first pregnancy and they didn't want her to be alone in the US. It made sense. The only problem Chika had was having to be at home since she had stopped working.

"Oh, but you can work at Safe Travels so you aren't always at home," Belinda, Samuel's wife, suggested. "Or you can join mummy and I at the dry-cleaning firm."

Although the dry-cleaning firm was less than five years old, it was already one of the leaders in Lagos. When they started, they offered new customers three months of free services and by the end of the third month, those customers stayed with them.

Chika didn't want to work in any of the family's businesses, but her mother-in-law convinced her that her sewing and fabric knowledge would be of great help.

It didn't take very long for Chika to realise Ugochi was right. She should have waited. The events that unfolded before her eyes got her depressed. She sank so deep into a pit of depression she couldn't climb out.

There was nothing to grasp unto for help. Not even her husband could save her.

Chapter Nine

When they moved into the duplex, it was with a lot of expectation. She knew in a matter of months a baby would be in the house.

When a scan revealed she was having twins, the whole family had been excited and even had a dinner celebration at the family house. She was speechless from the gifts she received from Samson's family. She saw how delighted his parents were and Chika was happy and silently prayed that Belinda and Samuel will experience what she and Samson were experiencing.

"Don't worry, I will help you fix up the nursery," Belinda smiled at her. "You don't have to lift a finger to do anything. It will be my pleasure to do this."

And true to her words, Belinda did and Chika would every day walk into her twins' nursery and imagine them in the room. She imagined them all over the house.

She was pampered by everyone.

One morning, the ringing of her phone woke her up. It was her sister Ugochi who called to pray with her because she had a bad dream. "Be prayerful Chika. I have been deeply disturbed in my spirit concerning you and I don't know why."

Chika told her she was fine. She knew her sister meant well, but since Ugochi joined a praying women's ministry after she got married, Ugochi became a prayer warrior and turned everything into a spiritual affair.

Hours later that same day, while at her routine antenatal checkup, the doctor sent her for a scan. Chika called her husband who was waiting in the car for her so they could go in together and see their identical boys on the machine. The sonographer excused himself after a few minutes and returned with her doctor who took a look at the machine and faced them.

Chika and Samson saw she was concerned and Chika grabbed Samson's hand.

"I'm sorry," Dr. Ronke said.

"What is it?" Samson asked.

"This is unexpected, but there's no heartbeat," the doctor said. She had noticed in her office when she tried to listen to the heartbeats of the babies with her stethoscope, that was why she sent Chika for a scan.

THE DELIVERANCE

"What do you mean there's no heartbeat?" Chika asked. "Aren't they supposed to be breathing in the womb?"

The doctor sighed. Samson understood what the doctor meant but Chika did not.

"I'm sorry Chika, but your twins have gone back to God."

It took a few more seconds for Chika to understand. "They are dead?" she looked at Samson, whose face was buried in his palm. "But, but ... how…"

Chika felt the cold hit her as she tried to process what she'd been told. She touched her belly. Rubbed it. Her babies were in there.

Samson called his parents and within the hour, the whole family was in the hospital but Chika was oblivious to what was going on. How could they have been dead for a week? She asked herself.

The doctors talked to her and Samson but Chika didn't understand anything they said. Induce labour. Deliver the babies. Burial?

Chika couldn't decide on anything or respond to questions. Her mother-in-law and Samson had to make all the decisions.

Three days later, when Chika walked back into her home, she felt empty. The excitement that came with moving into the house was gone. For long hours, she stayed in the nursery.

Samson, while dealing with his pains, also had to think of his wife. Chika said she couldn't stay in the house. She wanted to go home to Enugu to her parents and that was what she did.

When Chika returned to her house in Lagos, Stella, Samson's only sister, had moved into the duplex to help them cope with the recent loss. Chika thought nothing of it. They were only concerned about her wellbeing.

Two weeks into her stay with them, Stella walked into the nursery to watch Chika packing up some few gifts that had been opened the time they celebrated at the family house.

"What will you do with all these?" Stella asked.

"Keep them for the next baby, by the grace of God," Chika answered.

Stella didn't say anything for a while. "That was what Belinda said."

Chika looked at her. "What do you mean?"

"The baby gifts," Stella swept her hand through the air to indicate. "Most of the gifts came from Belinda's house. I think she was tired of seeing them as they reminded her of her losses."

THE DELIVERANCE

Chika stopped what she was doing. "How do you mean?"

"Belinda has had two miscarriages. She and my brother bought a lot of things when she was pregnant the first time. Everything is here in this room. They were generous right?" Stella asked.

Chika had no reply. She didn't know Belinda and Samuel had two losses. She only thought they hadn't gotten pregnant yet. She thought she saw a smirk on Stella's face, but it was gone as quickly as it appeared.

When Chika asked Samson about it, he said he didn't realise they were the same things and Chika believed him. She didn't know how to feel about knowing Belinda had packed up her nursery from next door and installed it in her house.

"It doesn't mean anything Chika," Ugochi told her. "It was actually nice of her to do that. Some people see it as sowing seeds into the kind of blessings they also want."

That evening, when Belinda returned from work, Chika went next door to hug and thank her. Then Chika apologised for reminding her about what she went through.

"I feel fine physically, Belinda," Chika told her, "but I'm not over it. Will I be fine?"

Belinda looked at her for a few seconds in silence before nodding. "Of course, Chika. This is between you and me okay? Why is Stella still in your house?"

Chika opened her mouth and closed it because she didn't know how to respond.

"Find a way to get her out," Belinda was serious. "I promise you she didn't just come to keep you company. She came to stay. Don't be stupid with this family. I'm done talking about it."

Chika was lost for words.

Chapter Ten

Chika's very short conversation with Belinda confused her. She found out too much information in one day. She wondered why nobody told her before Belinda had two losses. She hoped it wasn't a family thing. She also wondered about Stella.

Chika had always admired their relationship. Stella and Belinda behaved like best friends but with what Belinda told her, and the expression on her face when she said it, Chika was no longer sure.

What she noticed about Stella was that she liked to be in control of everything around her. Just like her mother-in-law, which wasn't exactly a bad thing. But after what Belinda said, she wondered if there was more to it.

She began to notice subtle things she didn't ordinarily pay attention to, especially during the weekends when they were all home. Stella always found a way to call Samson away from Chika's side or she would invite herself into their conversations.

Stella's friends frequented the house on weekends and at times, they stayed the night. Nobody asked her permission.

"Will your sister-in-law agree?" Chika had overheard one conversation.

"I don't need her permission. It's my father's house," Stella had responded.

Chika was about to go downstairs when she heard it. Stella and her friend had been having lunch downstairs. Chika had returned to her room worried as it dawned on her that her sister-in-law was there to stay.

"This is not right," she told herself. Though they had been married for six months at the time, her marriage was still very young and didn't need any form of interference.

She knew that a new marriage is like a new baby brought into the world. The baby is home with the family for the first few years of its life; family values, relationships and ethics are all instilled in him before he is sent into the world and exposed to different ideas and cultures. But because of the foundation and principles gotten from the family, that growing child is well-grounded to repel things that are dangerous to everything he has been raised to hold dear.

That was how she viewed a new marriage. Even their marriage counselling classes had said the same thing. A new marriage is an offspring from two families that should plant itself separately, be tended and its roots allowed to anchor so the home cannot be displaced by external forces.

And she got it wrong from the beginning because she and her husband didn't have that. First, Samuel and Belinda were next door. Though Samuel didn't come over to their wing often, Samson went next door every Saturday and Sunday so they could watch football together.

Chika hadn't seen anything wrong with it until she put everything in perspective when Belinda drew her attention to Stella.

Don't be stupid with this family. What did Belinda mean?

"Hey baby," Chika and her husband were together in their bedroom one Saturday morning. "Your sister has been here more than a month. When is she going back home?"

Samson looked at her. "Didn't I tell you?"

"Tell me what?"

"She's staying with us now."

Chika sat up in bed. "Why?"

Samson shrugged. "I guess she wants a change. Perhaps to be close to Samuel and me.

Chika chuckled. "You all work at the head office and see each other often enough."

Samson took her hand. "Please. Stella had always wanted to leave home to be alone but my parents will never allow her because she isn't married. They monitor her movements like a teenager. The closest thing she has to being herself and free is being here with us. This way, dad and mum know Samuel and I are watching out for her."

"So why didn't she stay next door?" Chika asked. Samuel was the older brother after all.

Samson raised both hands. "Whether she's here or next door, makes no difference. We are all under the same roof still."

Chika knew there was nothing she could say about it that wouldn't make her look bad. The best she could hope for was that Stella would get married as soon as possible and while they were living together, Chika would ensure they had no problems.

She was so engrossed in her job at the dry-cleaning firm that it didn't occur to her that she wasn't given an employment letter and she wasn't on salary. One afternoon, she overheard two staff in customer care discussing the cut in another staff's salary and realised she had worked three months without receiving a salary.

When she asked Belinda, her fear was realised. They worked the same way at the dry-cleaning firm as they did at Safe Travels. The family members weren't on salary because they had access to the accounts.

"So, you have access to the company's account too?" Chika asked her.

Belinda chuckled. "No, my husband takes care of all my needs and Samson should do the same for you," Belinda told her. "Hey, don't worry. Just be happy, and enjoy your life and you will have no problems."

Chika smiled. But, when she got home, she had a serious talk with Samson to find out if he was finally on salary. Negative. The family took care of all their needs and paid all their bills. It was never going to change.

Chika felt she had walked into a trap. She realised it was the reason Samson walked away from it all. To be free to be himself. It was a subtle manipulation that they understood but nobody could challenge.

She knew she didn't make any mistake marrying Samson because she loved him, but the family situation wasn't one she could turn her eyes away from. Belinda seemed to have adjusted to it. She didn't think she could do it. She had her own dreams and it was time she realised them.

The only reason she had kept off going for her training was because she had been pregnant. She believed it was the right time to go. But she didn't want to be away from Samson for so long.

She knew they could travel together for their courses. Samson had also not done anything towards realising his dreams since he returned to the family.

One night, she talked to her husband and reminded him of their dreams.

"I miss the days before we got married," he surprised her. "And we need to start with you. You have to leave my mum's company and focus on your fashion, babe. Remember you can always start with what you have right?"

Chika smiled.

"You have your sewing machine. If you need some more equipment, let's get them for you. Perhaps you could take a training course here in Lagos to learn something new. What do you think? Because I don't want you so far away from me and I know we can't go together."

Chika's heart was full of joy. She kissed him. He was the caring Samson she met at Oshodi one time.

"Mum's not going to like that you're leaving the company. But I will talk to her okay?"

She smiled at him.

"I am sorry," he apologised.

"For what?"

THE DELIVERANCE

He smiled wanly. "Was this the life you expected when you agreed to marry me?"

"Well," she started honestly. "Other than your sister in the house, and working without being paid," she added and they both laughed. "I think I'm good."

"And happy?" he asked her.

She nodded. "I was worried about you, the whole family sharing everything and having the same purse, but as long as I'm sure that you are here to look out for me, I'm happy."

He stroked her face. "Belinda is not happy," he told her. "I don't want you to become that. So, you will leave the company and start working on your dreams. That is what I want for you."

Chika sighed happily.

Fight for your marriage like it's under attack from the powers of hell; because it is!

— www.adivineencounter.com

Chapter Eleven

It was three weeks after Chika left her mother-in-law's company and started her training at a fashion house in Ikeja. Those three weeks had been very trying for her. Every time Stella saw her, she raised the topic. And Stella suddenly started inviting the whole family over on Sundays for family lunch, as she called it.

The first Sunday, two days after Chika resigned from the dry-cleaning company, Chika and Samson returned from church and met Mr and Mrs Omoefe, Solomon, Samuel and Belinda in the house.

"I think it is a good idea we start having lunch as a family together every Sunday. Stella told Samson before smiling at Chika. "Don't worry Chika, you don't have to do a thing. I will order food."

That was the day Chika realised Stella was out for her. Later, while they were seated at the dining table, Mr Omoefe asked Chika what her plans were now that she was jobless.

"I'm not exactly jobless, sir," Chika smiled. "I am doing a training."

"To be a common tailor," Stella added. "But I think your people like all this petty work. That's why they call your work Obioma right?"

Chika bit her tongue to hold her words in.

"If this is what you are sure you want to do, we will support you," her mother-in-law said. "We can carve out an office for you at the company. After all, we have all the sewing equipment you need."

"Oh, that is a great idea," the husband smiled and turned to Chika. "That way you don't have to worry about renting a place to work from."

"Thanks, mum," Samson quickly put in. "Chika doesn't need an office yet. She has a six-month training to do."

They finished lunch in silence and moved to the sitting room to watch movies. Samuel, Samson and Solomon excused themselves and went next door to Samuel's place to watch football. And Chika was about to go upstairs when her mother-in-law called her back.

"We love you like a daughter, Chika," she started. "We want you to be happy, like Belinda here. She's a good girl and we've never had any problems since she joined the family. Maybe in your family, you people do things differently. But here, we like to do everything together in

THE DELIVERANCE

unity. That is how we raised our children. Then you came in and all of a sudden, my son is acting strange. This family's strength is unity and nobody can break it. Whoever does not like how we do things here can leave. Remember Samson left before and he came back right? So, it is up to you to decide if you want to be a part of this unity."

Chika saw the smirk on Stella's face. Her father-in-law was pretending to be watching TV and Belinda was inspecting her beautiful nails. Her mother-in-law was still looking at her, waiting.

Chika smiled. "Thank you, mummy."

"Be wise, Chika, and be a good girl," her mother-in-law added.

"I will, ma."

The woman smiled and turned to the television and Chika escaped to her room. She understood everything her mother-in-law said and didn't say.

"So, you are keeping to this your stupidity," her mother-in-law said the following Sunday at the family lunch Stella invited everyone to again. Like the week before, the sons left for Samuel's place.

"I thought after we spoke on Sunday, you will return to work, but I didn't see you during the week."

"I started my training ma," Chika said.

The woman faced her daughter. "Didn't you tell me it is only three times a week she goes for the training?"

Stella nodded. "Yes, mum."

She turned to Chika. "So why can't you come the other days of the week that you are not going for that training?"

"I bring work home with me that I work on," Chika said. That was the agreement she had with her boss.

"Oh, you are working in this house?"

"She has a sewing machine in that room," Stella pointed.

"Hmmm."

Later when Chika was leaving them to retreat to her room upstairs, Stella called her.

"By the way, my car is at the mechanic. I will be using yours this week."

"Okay," Chika said.

Chika had been using the Rav 4 her parents-in-law gave them as a wedding gift, while Samson still used his Camry. Stella didn't ask to borrow it, she said she will use it. She didn't need Chika to agree. There were other cars to pick from at her parents' place if Stella wanted, but Chika understood the plan. A week later, she saw Stella's car in the compound but not the Rav 4. When she asked Stella, her sister-in-law smiled.

"It's with Mum, you can get it from her. Besides, the car is not exactly yours since Dad and Mum bought it, right?"

"Right," Chika agreed and smiled.

Chika didn't know how to handle the situation. She didn't care about the car, but she knew her husband's family was on a mission to frustrate her. Was it just Stella and the mum or everyone? The women were the vocal ones. She didn't know if the men were a part of it. She knew her husband wasn't happy about what was going on. He didn't ask her how her time with his parents went those Sundays he went next door with his brothers, but she knew he suspected. She was sure Belinda must have told her husband.

Even Belinda wasn't any kind of support. She minded her business and smiled whenever it was required of her or said Yes ma or Yes sir to their parents-in-law's demands.

She was having breakfast one morning when Stella came to join her. She didn't respond to Chika's greeting.

"You haven't been married one year, you are already dividing the family," Stella said looking at her. "Mum's been very nice to you. She loves you like a daughter too but you insist on using your hands to destroy your marriage."

Wisdom cautioned Chika not to say a word.

"You want to be a common tailor and, in your mind, that's better than managing a prestigious dry-cleaning firm. Imagine the opportunities you have there. The calibre of people you get to meet. And you throw it all away to be an Obioma. What a degrading job. Be wise. It's not too late. Mum will take you back."

Chapter Twelve

Chika was patient. Their dreams were her strength. She finished her training and her boss begged her to come on board as a designer in the fashion house. They serviced high calibre clients and the salary was good. After discussing it with her husband, Chika agreed to a one-year contract. Other than her salary, she got a percentage for her original designs that were used and Chika has a catalogue of designs.

She was on the right path towards realising her dreams. But the home was a prison. After Stella first took her car, Samson offered to drop her off at Ikeja but Chika refused.

"I was doing public transport before I met you," she told him.

"You are my wife now," Samson insisted.

So, every morning she went to Ikeja, he dropped her off before going to work and Chika used a cab back home. But after Stella deliberately left the car at her in-law's place, so Chika would ask her mother-in-law for it, Samson gave her his car and settled for using a cab. Eventually, almost two months after Samson gave her his car, one Sunday, when they came for the family lunch, the Rav 4 was returned.

"This car is taking space in my compound," her mother-in-law told her as she dropped the key in front of Chika. "Why haven't you come to carry it since instead of collecting my son's car?"

Chika didn't know how to reply, so she thanked her.

When she finished her training, she invited the whole family to the dinner organised by the fashion house to celebrate the new graduates. While most of the others had trained for a year, Chika and two others trained for six months because they already had some knowledge.

To her surprise, the whole family came and Samson, who had come prepared to document his wife's day, was happy to document the entire event when he realised no photographer was secured to do it.

"You didn't tell me your husband is a photographer," Nikky, her boss, said. "And your in-laws, girl…" Nkiru smiled and shook her head.

The Sunday after that dinner, when they came to the house for family lunch, Chika gave each person a top she made for them. She didn't need their measurement as she had eyes for telling people's sizes, so she used the international standard measurement for their sizes.

THE DELIVERANCE

"This is so thoughtful of you, thank you very much," Belinda said smiling.

Chika saw her mother-in-law look at Belinda quietly for a few seconds. "Yes, thank you," the woman finally said. "You shouldn't have bothered though. I like my clothes already made."

"So, my dear," it was her father-in-law. "Now that you are done with the training, what are your plans for the future for work? You know you must work and contribute to running the home. There's no free bed or free food anywhere. Or were you paid while you were training?"

"Nobody pays an apprentice, daddy," Stella took over. "She was the one that paid plenty money to be an apprentice. Good money the family would have used for something better."

Chika realised they thought Samson paid her training fees. She turned to look at him.

"Chika saved that money from her salary for two years while she was working, before we got married. I knew she always wanted to do this."

There was a moment of silence before her father-in-law asked her again what her plans were.

"Oh, she can just return to the company instead of sitting at home," her mother-in-law smiled at her. "There are lots of benefits. You can have better opportunities to help your family advance in life."

Stella nodded. "That is a good idea. That is if she wants to."

"You were going for training three times a week and using the rest of your days to work from home, right?" her mother-in-law asked and Chika nodded. "Do the same. Come to the company three times a week and use the other days to work from home."

"Chika is still going to Nikky. She was given full-time employment. Every day of the week," Samson told his mother.

Chika sighed. "I haven't accepted the offer," she lied. "I can come back to the company."

"No!" Samson said.

Nobody said anything after that. After lunch, Samson didn't go next door with his brothers. He told the others he and Chika were going out to visit friends.

They didn't go out to visit friends. They went out to be alone by themselves.

When Chika resumed work at Nikky as an employee, she handed over the CD containing the pictures from the dinner night. Samson had edited them over the weekend.

THE DELIVERANCE

Nikky was really pleased to see the beautiful pictures. "Does he work as a photographer?" she asked Chika.

"It's his dream."

"Well let him start. My friend is 50 this weekend and we are throwing her a surprise party. Ask if he is available to cover it and let's know his fees."

Samson hadn't covered any event since Ugochi's wedding. After Chika started her training, he took three different online courses important to developing his skill. The dinner had been his only opportunity of doing some work. When she told him, Samson was excited.

"I think we have to figure out a way to advertise your services so clients can start booking you," Chika said.

All of a sudden, things were happening fast. From the surprise birthday party, Samson got two other engagements and had to travel to Abuja for one. Chika saw her husband change. He became more alive. He went to work at Safe Travels happy, returned home and got on his system to do personal work.

Nikky turned out to be a fairy godmother. As clients poured through the Nikky showroom, she offered photography services for their events and for every job she secured for Samson, Nikky took a fair percentage. Samson didn't mind. He was just happy to be doing what he really wanted.

One day he presented his father with a catalogue of Safe Travels, showcasing their offices in some of the states, their minibuses, cars, and luxurious buses, and the interior.

It was a beautiful catalogue he worked on for over three months. Despite everything, Chika knew how much Samson loved his family and wanted so much for them to accept his choices. He just wanted that acknowledgement from his father. He didn't plan to leave Safe Travels, but he wanted to be able to satisfy his family and still fulfil his dreams.

"So?" Chika asked. She wanted to know how her father-in-law reacted to the surprise catalogue.

Samson shrugged. "He flipped through and dropped it."

Her heart broke. Her husband was disappointed.

Three months before their second wedding anniversary, Chika was about to leave the house for work when Stella met her outside.

"This madness has gone on long enough," Stella started. "It is your business if you decide to become a common tailor, making clothes for people who shouldn't even be up to your standard as a member of this family, but it is another thing if you drag my brother down this road with you to become a photographer to be snapping common people."

"These same common people are the ones that patronize Safe Travels," Chika answered her. "Imagine if they were all flying, who will enter Safe Travels?"

They held gazes. Chika knew she shouldn't have said that, but how long could she keep quiet?

"I'll make sure you don't forget what you just said," Stella told her before turning to go back into the house. At the door, she paused and looked at Chika. "You seem to forget you don't have any children for us yet. So, there are no strings attached. Don't get too comfortable."

Where you are today is no accident. God is using the situation you are in right now to shape you and prepare you for the place He wants to bring you into tomorrow. Trust Him with His plan even if you don't understand it.

— Daughterbydesign.wordpress.com

Chapter Thirteen

Chika asked herself if that was the day her marriage ended. She went to work offended by Stella's words. The whole day, she tried to reach Samson on the phone but his line was switched off. He wasn't home when she got back from work. His line was still switched off.

With no other choice, she asked Stella, who hissed without responding. Unsure of what to do, Chika went next door to ask Samuel if he saw Samson at work.

"Go to your house, Chika," he said. "Samson is fine and will come home."

Chika wanted to say more but thought better of it. She didn't see Belinda. Back at their wing of the duplex, Chika fretted. Finally, she called her father-in-law but it was the wife that answered the phone.

"What do you want?"

"Good evening ma," Chika started. "I wanted to ask Dad if he saw Samson at work."

"Didn't Samuel already tell you he is fine and will come home whenever he wants? Goodnight."

Chika looked at the phone in her hand. What was going on? She needed to talk to someone, so she called Ugochi. It was almost 11:00 p.m.

Her sister listened to her and calmed her down. They prayed together and Ugochi convinced her to go to bed. It took her a while to fall asleep. When she woke up in the middle of the night, she breathed a sigh of relief to see her husband sleeping by her side.

Chika put her arm around him, rested her face behind his neck and fell asleep.

When she got downstairs in the morning and greeted him with a kiss, the man who looked like her husband, sounded like him and wearing his clothes, was a stranger. He looked at her, but it felt like he looked through her.

Chika felt something huge fall in the middle of her chest.

"I looked for you yesterday," she told him. "Are you feeling okay?" she used the back of her hand to feel his forehead but Samson withdrew from her touch. He wore a look of irritation on his face which shocked her. Chika heard a noise and turned to see Stella looking at her. She had a satisfied smirk on her face. "Good morning," Chika greeted.

Stella frowned. "Seriously? Is it really a good morning?"

THE DELIVERANCE

Chika looked from her to Samson who won't look at her. "Let me quickly get your breakfast ready," she told her husband and headed into the kitchen, past Stella, who turned and followed her and watched her slice onion and tomatoes as she made scrambled eggs.

When Chika was done, Stella left the kitchen to sit at the dining table where her brother was to wait for Chika to serve the food.

Chika dropped the tray in front of Samson and looked at Stella. "Are you ready for breakfast too?"

Stella looked at her and smiled without saying a word.

Chika felt uneasy. "Babe," she addressed her husband who was reading a newspaper article on his iPad. Chika touched him and he looked up. She noticed that look in his eyes again. He didn't recognise her. "Your breakfast is in front of you," she pointed.

Samson looked at the tray and shook his head. "Not hungry," he mumbled and returned his focus to the iPad.

"Samson," Stella called. "Should I make you something else to eat?"

Samson looked at his sister and Chika noticed the annoyance that crept into his eyes. He pushed the chair back. "I'm off to work."

Chika followed him outside. "Babe, are you okay?"

He was by his car and backing her. "I don't know."

Chika swallowed hard and laid her hand flat on his back. "What's wrong?" she heard him sigh deeply then he turned to face her. And within a split second, Chika saw the confusion on his face turn into something else when he looked beyond Chika. She turned and Stella was standing by the entrance, looking at the both of them.

Samson turned back, opened his car door and got in. Chika watched him drive out of the compound and felt she should have jumped into the car with him. When she turned to go back into the house, Stella wasn't there.

Chika endured the worse month of her life. Her husband was lost somewhere and she didn't know how to reach him. When he looked at her, it was with confusion and a lack of recognition. Since the day he became a stranger, Samson stopped eating her meals. He turned down her breakfasts. Every day, he came home late, when he was sure Chika would be in bed. Samson returned from work and stayed next door with Samuel and Belinda. He ate his meals there too.

Chika was confused. She didn't understand what was going on. Her sister-in-law strutted around the house feeling victorious over what Chika couldn't comprehend. The Sunday family lunch tradition continued and became a nightmare for her because Chika felt she was being taunted. She could tell they watched her body language, especially when she and Samson stopped sitting together at the table.

After lunch, her husband still disappeared with his brothers and Chika would retreat to their bedroom to escape the sarcasm and clothed insults directed at her and her family.

It had become a constant thing. She couldn't understand why Samson's family suddenly felt they had to show off to her.

"Has your father travelled out of the country before?" her father-in-law asked her. "This is a once-in-a-lifetime opportunity for your parents to experience the good life. Will you tell them I am inviting them?"

That day, Chika had smiled and said nothing.

She felt choked as if she were in a prison. Her best times of the day were at work. Every time she came home, she picked up the jacket of gloom she left outside when she left the house.

Stella was in charge of her home. The sitting room, the TV, and the kitchen were hers. She entertained her friends. The only place she didn't make Chika feel unwanted was in her bedroom.

Several times, she considered telling Ugochi and seeking advice, but Chika couldn't. She didn't want her family to know what she was going through. She couldn't even tell the only two friends she had. They wouldn't believe her story. They never stopped telling her how lucky she was to have married Samson. Chika was looking for the best approach to her problems. Maybe she should leave Nikky and join the dry-cleaning firm for peace to reign.

The third Sunday after Samson became a stranger, Chika had excused herself early from the table that she wasn't feeling well and escaped to her room. She was standing by the window trying to understand how she allowed herself to get to where she was when she heard the door open. She didn't bother to turn around. She knew Samson would have gone next door by that time. So, his mother or sister had come up to provoke her. They wanted Chika provoked enough to reply them with words they could use against her.

"You said you aren't feeling well."

Chika turned around at the unexpected voice. It was her husband. He was inspecting something on the rug. "My love?" Chika wanted to touch his face but she was afraid. He pulled away from her touches. But she wanted so much to do it. "I wasn't comfortable downstairs." She was going to say she wasn't comfortable with his family but decided against it.

"Me too," he said. It was almost a whisper but she caught it. Chika swallowed. He was still downcast. Then she did it. She lifted her hand and just placed her palm against his

THE DELIVERANCE

cheek. She was ready for his withdrawal but he didn't move. Samson raised his head and she noticed his eyes were closed but she saw the tears and he rubbed his face more against her palm and Chika closed the distance and pulled her husband into her arms.

He held her too. And tightly. "I miss you," he whispered. "I thought I lost you. Please don't leave me."

Despite everything she wanted to say, everything she didn't understand, Chika remained quiet and just enjoyed a rare moment, the first with her husband in almost a month.

"Samson!"

Chika felt him tense up in her arms and he quickly stepped away from her. His mother was standing in the doorway.

"Samuel and Solomon are waiting for you to go watch football," the woman said to her son but her eyes were on Chika.

And he left, without a glance at her.

"I thought you said you weren't feeling fine," her mother-in-law asked her gently. "You should be resting my dear." She closed the door and Chika was left standing there perplexed.

"What just happened?" she asked herself as she dropped on the bed and buried her face in her hands, shaking from silent sobs.

She didn't know when she fell asleep but she woke up when Samson got into bed and put his arms around her. The room was dark and she was still dressed in her church clothes.

"Hey love," he kissed her. "I didn't mean to wake you up."

Chika wanted to sit up, but he stopped her. "I need to get off these clothes and I am hungry. What time is it?"

"Just 8:00 p.m."

Chika stretched. "I didn't get to say goodbye to your parents."

"That's fine," he said and apologised for leaving the way he did earlier. "It's just that, I don't know what's happening to me. And I feel I'm hurting you a lot, but I don't know how," he kept quiet. "Am I hurting you, babe?"

Chika knew they were continuing from where they stopped in the afternoon. "Honestly, I don't know," and it was the truth. "And we've spoken more to each other today than in the last three weeks."

"I noticed. Why is that?" he asked. "Did I do something? Were you mad at me?"

"No, baby, but it doesn't matter anymore now that we are here." And she kissed him. Although she didn't understand what was happening, she was going to make sure the last three weeks do not repeat themselves.

Later they fell asleep in each other's arms. She woke up early and went downstairs to find something to eat. A smile played across her face when she remembered the night before. Everything was going to be alright, she told herself.

Chika was finishing her breakfast when Samson came downstairs. He was dressed for work.

"Morning sweetheart," she scrambled to her feet and rushed to plant a big kiss on his lips. "Let me get your breakfast," she turned and was leaving for the kitchen.

"No."

Chika stopped and turned to face him and she saw it again and her heart dropped. Samson was looking at her as if he was trying to remember who she was. "Samson?"

He shook his head. "No breakfast, thank you."

She watched him walk away with her heart twisted tight.

"Looks like you guys are having marital issues."

Chika didn't notice Stella at the foot of the stairs.

"Sorry," Stella said. "I have been noticing it for some weeks now. I hope this is not heading for divorce o. For better, for worse. Have a nice day. I'm riding with my brother."

Chika watched her leave.

Chapter Fourteen

The days that followed that morning, Samson didn't come home. He stayed at his parents' place, according to Stella. Chika also noticed some of his clothes and personal belongings were gone. She assumed Samson must have come home during the day to pack some things.

Every time she called his number, it was switched off. Then one time, Stella posted on Instagram a picture of herself, her friend and Samson. They must have gone out. Stella's friend and Samson were laughing over something, which shocked Chika. Her husband was laughing. She couldn't remember the last time she laughed. She couldn't remember the last time she heard her husband laugh.

The next morning, she woke up early and drove to her in-laws' place to see her husband.

"This is quite a surprise, my dear," her father-in-law said to her after answering her greetings. "We don't see you here often enough."

"I'm sorry about that sir," she apologised.

"I assume you are here to see your husband."

"Yes sir."

"Go on, he is upstairs getting ready for work."

Chika found him in his old bedroom. "Hey."

"Chika?" it was a question. "Why are you here?" he was looking at her through the mirror as he wore his belt.

She walked up to him. "That's what I want to know. Why are you here?" she asked him. He turned to face her. They stared at each other quietly, then he shrugged.

"I'm sorry. I just needed to be alone to think," he said.

"Away from me?" she asked.

He didn't say anything.

She turned to leave. "I shouldn't have come."

"Babe," he caught her hand.

"You left without saying a word to me. I cannot reach you on the phone. Nine days today."

"I'm doing this for us," he said.

Chika nodded. "Of course."

THE DELIVERANCE

"Should I take you to work?" he surprised her. "I miss doing that," he smiled at her.

Chika could only look at him, unsure of what to say. "I drove over, don't bother." She didn't want to be angry, but she was. "Excuse me," Chika walked out of the room.

Chika found her mother-in-law behind the building doing her every morning stretches.

"Good morning Mum," she greeted.

"My dear, Dad said you were around. How are you?"

"I'm fine ma," Chika replied and wondered again how the woman wore many personas. Chika couldn't find any sarcasm or any body language that suggested anything different from the words of her mother-in-law as they chatted briefly before Chika excused herself and left.

Chika could not work the whole day. The wave of fatigue and headache that had been plaguing her the last few days returned. It was usually worse in the afternoons, that Chika would sit still for almost thirty minutes before she felt better.

But that day, her boss, Nikky, insisted she go to the hospital. After the spell passed, Chika left for the hospital, the same one the family uses because they were already registered there. An hour after she arrived, the doctor called her back into his office and congratulated her.

"10 weeks," he said.

"10 weeks what?"

"You're 10 weeks pregnant."

Chika smiled faintly. She couldn't process her feelings. Was she going to bring a child into her current environment? Where she was not wanted unless she bent to the wishes of her in-laws?

Chika called Ugochi when she got back into the car. "Am I sensing concern in your voice?" her sister asked.

Chika hesitated. "I think I need to travel for a week or two. Maybe I should go to Enugu to see Mum and Dad, then come to Abuja to see my nephew."

"And me," Ugochi nodded.

"Of course," Chika smiled, suddenly feeling better.

When she got home, she called her boss and asked for two weeks off.

Before she left the following day, Chika sent a message to Samson informing him of her trip.

When the plane touched down and she turned on her phone, she saw a message from Samson.

THE DELIVERANCE

"Please call me," the message read.

Chika did not. She came home to her parents. Whatever issues she had, she left them behind in Lagos and travelled light. She didn't want anything to spoil her good mood. Quickly, she replied to his message.

"Not now, please."

When she got to her parents' house, Chika wasn't surprised to learn that her mother-in-law had gone ahead of her to complain Chika didn't tell anyone she was travelling. "How can she come to Enugu empty-handed and not allow me to send good greetings to my in-laws?" her mother-in-law had lamented on the phone to her mother. Then her mother looked at her and asked if she was sure everything was alright.

Chika smiled and hugged her mother. "Everything is getting better," she cooed. "I'm pregnant."

And that announcement ended the trail of questions that would have followed.

She spent four peaceful days in Enugu, visited with her siblings who lived there, before flying to Abuja to be with Ugochi.

"When was the last time you spoke with him?" Ugochi asked immediately after she got into the car. She had insisted on picking Chika up from the airport.

"A day before I left Lagos."

Ugochi put the key in the ignition but did not turn it. "There is more that you aren't telling me, right?"

Chika shrugged. What could she tell Ugochi? How would she explain the true situation of things, that her husband's mother and sister, maybe his whole family, were on a mission to end her marriage and Samson was a willing party?

"Yes," she answered finally. "But I'd rather not talk about it. At least not now."

"Is your life threatened?"

Chika smiled. "No."

"Good," Ugochi replied and finally started the car. "Else, I would get home and I will kick him out of my house."

It took a while for Chika to understand what her sister said. "Wait. What?"

"Your husband is here. He came in last night."

Chika sighed. She didn't know what to say.

They drove on silently for a while. "He told me things," Ugochi started. "He did. But he wasn't making any sense.

THE DELIVERANCE

He seemed very sad. He said he's hurt you a lot, and he doesn't know why or how."

"I wish you told me he was here. I wouldn't have come," Chika said. "Did you also tell him I am pregnant?"

"No, but he knows."

The doctor, Chika thought, must have called her mother-in-law with the news.

Samson was outside waiting for them and went to open the passenger door. "Babe," he looked at her. "Come here." He took her hand and helped her out of the car and into his arms.

Chika allowed herself to relax. "Samson," she started.

"No," he shook his head. "Let's get you settled in first. Ugo, thank you."

Ugochi nodded.

"You didn't need to come here," Chika said as he closed the door to the guest bedroom. "I was going to come back home."

"Oh, Chika my love," he pushed her hair back. "I know we haven't been in a good place. I think I have messed a lot up. I thought keeping you from getting entangled in my family's nest was the best thing for us. I do want you to be happy, to pursue your dreams."

"But?" she urged him on.

He shrugged. "I don't know. This is where it has brought us. You're unhappy and I am unhappy. But I love you, babe. That hasn't changed and that won't change. And I want us forever too."

She sighed. "Okay. Why did you leave the house?"

"Mum invited me to spend time with them."

"You could have told me something. Don't you think? And I couldn't reach you at all on your phone. And your sister…"

"My sister needs to leave the house," he said seriously and they looked at each other. "We are starting a family and we want a fresh start. Our second anniversary is around the corner."

"In two months," she said.

"Let's take a trip. Where do you want to go?"

Finally, she allowed herself to smile. If her husband was looking for a solution to the issues in their marriage, she should support him. "Anywhere you desire, as long as we get to be together and alone." She hooked her hands behind his neck. "And I love you Samson Omoefe. Like yesterday, like today and like tomorrow."

THE DELIVERANCE

Samson kissed his wife.

They spent three days in Abuja and returned to Lagos. The week that followed was pure bliss. Her husband was super attentive to her. He took her to work daily and returned to pick her up.

None of her in-laws had congratulated her on her pregnancy. She was aware they knew because it was her mother-in-law that informed Samson about the pregnancy. She noticed Samson avoided leaving her in the house alone. When they were home, they stayed upstairs in their bedroom. If she needed to prepare their meal, he stayed with her in the kitchen. As long as Stella was in the house, he never let Chika be alone.

She and Samson went to London, and then Paris for their second anniversary. By this time, she was past the fatigue and starting her fourth month of pregnancy. They were happy. They did a lot of shopping and Samson bought some gadgets for his photography and couldn't stop taking pictures of her.

After a hiatus on his social media photography pages, Samson was back to life and posting his pictures from their vacation.

Chika noticed the gradual return of the tension as they headed to the airport to return home.

"I wish we could stay here," Samson said. "The past three weeks were glorious."

Though she went for checkups regularly and the doctor assured her everything was on track, her in-laws wanted her to stop working.

"Don't stress yourself or the baby," her mother-in-law started. "A baby takes a lot of time so you should adjust and just be around the family who can help take care of you."

"She has me for that, Mum," Samson said.

"You are doing it again," his mother said, smiling at him.

"Doing what?" Samson was perplexed.

"Taking her side and defending her as if we want to harm her," she said without missing a beat.

"Mum?" Samson protested. And that was the end of that day's family lunch.

The next few weeks weren't better. Samson returned from work daily with complaints about how he was being treated by his family.

"Can you imagine I went to withdraw and all the accounts I have access to are without funds? I asked Stella and she asked me to talk to Dad. I finally asked to be placed on

THE DELIVERANCE

salary, especially now that we are having a baby and Dad said my annual salary wouldn't cover the rent of this duplex or our cars. He laughed though, and said it was a joke and promised to fund the empty accounts."

"I'm sorry," was all she could say.

In God's hands, nothing you go through gets wasted. Keep persevering, you have a purpose.

— Steven Furtick

Chapter Fifteen

And then came their princess. Becoming a mother made Chika joyful, elated, empowered, and all the emotions you can think about.

According to customs, a new mother and baby are cared for by an elderly woman for at least the first few days or weeks until the new mother is strong enough to care for herself and her baby. Usually, either the maternal or paternal grandmother of the new baby takes on this role.

When Chika had her baby, her mother came to Lagos the next day.

"You shouldn't have stressed yourself," her mother-in-law told her mother. "Chika is in good hands here."

"And I do not doubt it and I thank you so much for taking good care of my daughter. And congratulations again, we have a beautiful granddaughter."

When Chika was discharged, her mother-in-law insisted Chika and the baby stay at their place for the first few months. "I have to take care of my grandchild," her mother-in-law said.

"That's fine," her mother said. "I came to take care of my daughter too."

Other than Ugochi who had a slight idea of what Chika was going through, the rest of her family was unaware. Chika didn't want them to bother about her. But that day at the hospital, she knew her mother sensed something. Later when her mother was helping her with her bath and massaging her still protruded stomach with hot water, it came out.

"Tell me the truth, is everything fine?"

"No," she said truthfully. "But we are better now than before, so don't worry."

"Your husband, is he good to you?"

Chika nodded.

"So, it's the family again," her mother noted. Chika understood. Her mother was thinking of the time before they got married and how overbearing Samson's family had been.

THE DELIVERANCE

A day after the naming of her daughter, her mother told her she couldn't stay. Samson's mum looked for excuses to go into her room to look around as if expecting something to be missing. She made Chika's mum uncomfortable.

"Oh, my in-law, I would have served you this drink, but it is imported and my friends are coming to visit the baby. I have to serve them this drink."

"My in-law, are you watching this show? Let us watch something else."

"My in-law, we don't eat that kind of food in this house. Would you prefer an English breakfast instead?"

"My in-law, put your clothes in the wardrobe."

"My in-law, my granddaughter will be the most spoilt and pampered girl in the world. I and my husband will ensure we leave her a good inheritance, just as we did our children, you see. No need for them to struggle to find jobs or lack anything money can buy or struggle to pay rent. We have worked very hard to ensure even our fourth-generation children are financially secure. Isn't that wonderful?"

And all through, Chika's mum would only smile.

After her mother left, it didn't take long for frustration to set in because Chika felt helpless. Years later, she would realise what she dealt with after the birth of Sofia had a name. Postnatal depression.

Chika struggled with Sofia. Her mother-in-law didn't help her with the baby. Her mum had been the one attending to both mother and child. After she left, her mother-in-law said Chika must have learnt how to bathe the baby from her mother.

Twice, her mother-in-law reprimanded the maid for helping Chika with Sofia. "Did I employ you to be a nanny or to attend to my needs? Don't go near my grandchild."

It was unbelievable and Chika was sad. She couldn't even communicate what was happening with Samson because immediately after the naming, he went off to set up Safe Travels in three other states.

"Why can't the manager employed for that state, do his work?" Samson asked his father when the trip was mentioned. "I only have to be there for a day or two and return home."

His father wanted him to stay two weeks in each of the states to ensure a smooth handover. "And you have to go back every month to monitor their operations. You are the Operations Manager, this is your responsibility."

"Yes, Dad," he said. "Can't we do it the way we did the others? My baby and my wife need me."

THE DELIVERANCE

"We will be fine here," Chika chirped in. "Go and do your job."

Her father-in-law smiled thankfully at her.

Six weeks. Her husband was gone for six weeks. She remained in her in-laws' house alone with Sofia. She didn't know what to do with the baby who cried a lot. Even her in-laws kept asking her to shut the child up. All manner of thoughts invaded her mind. Not once did she not feel like filling the bathtub with hot water and just pushing Sofia under the water.

She was stressed, alone and helpless. She couldn't approach her mother-in-law for help because she didn't know what help she wanted. The last time she did, her mother-in-law smiled and told her it is a journey every woman took. "Don't worry dear, just take it easy, one day at a time." Encouraging words without the right action to back them up.

Her mother-in-law wouldn't take the baby off her even for a minute. She came in the morning and evening to peep at her and ask if everything was fine.

Chika couldn't wait for Samson's return. She wanted to go back home. And she wanted to return to work because she was tired of being at home. Two weeks before Samson's return, Chika got a maid. Iyanda, her friend and former colleague had helped her and even followed the maid over to her in-law's place.

They agreed the girl would resume immediately but she couldn't stay at her in-laws' place. So, Titi stayed with Iyanda but went daily to help Chika, pending when Chika went back home, and Titi could move in.

Her mother-in-law frowned at the arrangement. "Is that how your mother trained you? That you have to get a maid to raise your child? Didn't she teach you well?"

Chika had been shocked and speechless. Sophia stayed awake all night and Chika was stressed and tired.

"Just one baby and you are already spending our money on a maid?"

"Mum," Chika finally opened her mouth. "I have my own money. I work. I can pay for a maid. I am stressed and tired and I need help."

Then Samson returned, and it was time to move back to their place.

Chapter Sixteen

The man who left her and the one who returned was not her husband. Rather, he became a familiar stranger, one Chika encountered the weeks before discovering she was pregnant. He wouldn't look at her. He wouldn't talk to her. He wouldn't go near their daughter. At times, he slept next door with his brother.

Chika hardly saw him. He came only to get a change of clothes and was gone. Family Sunday lunch had stopped. Her mother-in-law told her Sophia needed all her attention so the family didn't come over on Sundays anymore. Family Sunday lunch was moved next door and Chika wasn't invited, which she was grateful for. Still, it disturbed her. Especially because they took her maid to attend to them next door. The same maid her mother-in-law frowned at. And Chika knew Belinda had a maid.

When Sofia turned three months, Chika returned to work. She couldn't stay a day more in the house without losing her mind. Nikky allowed her to bring Titi and Sophia with her the first week.

On Saturday, her mother-in-law came to visit them. "It's been a while since I saw my granddaughter," she said.

Chika had been feeding Sofia. Immediately after she was done, she took Sofia to her mother-in-law.

"No, it's okay. I have seen her now. She just finished eating so I don't want her to soil my clothes."

Chika smiled back. She could count the number of times her mother-in-law had held Sofia on the fingers of one hand.

"I heard you resumed work."

"Yes, mum," Chika sat down opposite her mother-in-law after strapping Sofia to the bouncer.

"Sofia is too young for that stress. Don't take my granddaughter out to work. And you are exposing her to strangers. There are wicked people everywhere."

"Mum, I have to go back to work."

"Chika, you can go to work," her mother-in-law said, "But leave the girl at home. Isn't that why you got a maid to help you raise your child since you cannot do it? I raised my four children alone. No maid. Ask Dad."

Samson came downstairs at that moment, on his way out.

"Samson," his mother started. "How can you allow your wife to go back to work with Sophia?"

THE DELIVERANCE

Samson looked at Chika. "Don't take the girl out of the house," he said and left.

"That settles it. If you won't listen to me, you have to listen to the father of your daughter. But if you must work and take the baby with you, your place at the company is still available. At least Sophia will be among family who are watching her, not some strangers. People will see you and think you are suffering, whereas you have everything," the woman paused. "You have been kicking against every help we want to give you. Don't you want your life to be better? Do you want to be like all your siblings who have to hustle daily for their bread? Look at you. You eat food you do not pay for. You live in this beautiful house you did not build. You drive a car you did not buy. Sofia gets all her supplies from the same purse. Haven't we done well for you? How many young couples have a house of their own? It took Dad and me a long time to make it and we planned our children's lives will be easier. But you are making Samson very sad. The least you could do is support this family, in whatever way you can. Did your family give you this kind of comfort?

"Mum," Chika controlled herself. "Please don't talk about my family."

"Hey!" Stella surfaced and clapped both hands. "You are talking back at my mother."

Her mother-in-law shook her head. "Your parents didn't train you well. If they did, you wouldn't have brought all these problems into my family when all we are trying to do is better your life. Don't you know when it is better for you, it will be better for your family?"

"It's Samson's fault, Mum," Stella said. "He is the one who didn't marry his class."

"Don't think we don't love you, Chika," Mum stood up.

Chika watched mother and daughter leave. She didn't know she was crying until her tears dropped on her hand.

That evening, Titi knocked on the bedroom door. "Madam, sorry ma, but I want to stop working."

Chika's heart missed a beat. "What? Why? Do I treat you bad?"

"No ma," Titi looked down. She told Chika she got another job and she couldn't refuse it because the salary was good and could give more assistance to her family.

"Where did this job come from? Have you been looking for a new job?"

"No ma. It's favour. God did it. Aunty Stella employed me to help Mummy and they doubled my salary."

Chika was speechless.

"I am starting on Monday."

"Congratulations," Chika said, boiling up inside. "So, you are leaving tomorrow?"

"Aunty Stella said I should stay here and be following Aunty Belinda to work."

Tell fearful souls, "Courage! Take heart! God is here, right here, on His way to put things right and redress all wrongs. He's on His way! He'll save you!"

— Isaiah 35:4

Chapter Seventeen

When Stella returned from going out with her mother, Chika was waiting for her in the living room.

"What are you doing please?" Chika started.

"Good evening to you too," Stella said.

"If you want somebody to help Mum, did it have to be my employee?"

Stella feigned surprise. "What's wrong with helping someone who needs help?"

"She works for me. She helps me, but you wanted to frustrate me, that's why you did this. And on top of that, you said she can stay."

"Chika, this is my father's house, in case you have forgotten. I have more rights here than you do. Don't think because you have one child for us, nothing can change. Any babe can have a child for my brother. You know the right thing to do but you refuse to do it. Don't complain." Stella finished and walked away.

Chika was rocking Sofia to sleep in the bedroom when Samson appeared in the doorway. Chika noticed he looked unsure and wondered why he was there. Since he decided to let his family ruin their lives and make her miserable, she had been taking it a day at a time, focused on her daughter.

"Did you have an altercation with Mum, and this evening with Stella?" he asked her.

Chika stopped walking to and fro and faced him. "Who said I did?"

"Babe, you need to apologise," Samson told her.

Chika frowned. Her being quiet had been taken for foolishness and naiveté. "Shouldn't you ask me first what happened?"

"It doesn't matter!" he spat, shocking her. Samson had never raised his voice at her. "Chika, if you want peace, go and apologise to them."

"I would rather leave this house today!" she dropped Sofia on the bed and went to stand in front of him. "How dare you, Samson. Is this the man I married?"

"The one you married? Obviously not," her mother-in-law was at the door. "Thank God I had not gone home. I was next door with Samuel when Stella came to meet us there.

THE DELIVERANCE

Chika, if you refuse to live in peace with us, you can just make up your mind."

Chika looked at her. Stella was beside her mother. "Make up my mind and do what?"

They looked at her.

"You want me to leave? Is that what this is all about? I should leave, right?"

Samson touched her. "Nobody said that, babe."

"Samson, leave her alone. She can do whatever she wants with her life," Stella said. "You can talk back to my mother. Talk to me however you want. Who do you think you are?"

Chika stared at her feet. This was it. Then she shook her head. "I don't think I can take this anymore," she said. "I don't know what I did to deserve this treatment, but I am tired," Chika cried and marched to the wardrobe doors. "I can't do this anymore, Lord."

She started to pick her things.

"Ha, you want to leave? Did anybody ask you to leave?" her mother-in-law asked. "It's your choice o. If you are going, go. But don't even think of taking my granddaughter anywhere or taking our car."

And she turned and left the room. Stella grabbed Samson by the hand and pulled him after her.

She collapsed on the bed and began to cry as she considered her life. How she ended up where she was. Her family was right. She should have taken enough time to know these people before marrying their son. She flung every caution away because she was in love. She ignored the wisdom of her family. She ignored Samson's reluctance to return. What did she do wrong? She wondered. Maybe she should have stood her ground and refused to move into the house. Maybe she shouldn't have encouraged Samson to return to Safe Travels. But were those faults hers? She didn't know whether or not she had a hand to play in everything that was happening to her.

She felt alone in the war being waged on her. It was her against the Omoefes. Samson wasn't helping her. He seemed unable to stand up for her. How could she win a battle that was already lost? She was at the end of her marriage, four months before her third wedding anniversary.

And there was Sophia, her innocent daughter. As much as she had a hard time coping with being a mother and understanding the different emotions that surged through her body, despite the postnatal depression that made her wish her baby wasn't existing because of her state of mind, Chika knew there was no way she could leave Sophia behind.

"Don't go with the child," her mother-in-law told her.

THE DELIVERANCE

The same child her mother-in-law doesn't care about. Stella had not picked up the baby once since she was born.

"Chika."

She looked up and saw Samuel in her room. Why? To continue from where the others stopped?

"Mum said you decided to leave. Is it true?"

"That is what your family wants, isn't it?" she asked him. With Samuel, Chika didn't know where he stood. He and Belinda found a way to cocoon themselves from the family and it worked for them.

He sighed. "What do you want?" he asked her.

"I don't know anymore."

"What did you want when you decided to marry my brother?" he asked.

Chika thought for a minute. "I just wanted to be happy and live in peace with the man I love. I had dreams. He had dreams. We wanted to achieve them together."

"Is it too late to achieve those?"

Chika dried her face and considered what he was saying and what he wasn't saying. "Please speak plainly with me. My head is confused."

"Right now, what is more important to you? The job or your marriage?"

Chika let her mouth hang open for a few seconds. "One makes me very happy and puts me on the path to achieving my dreams. The other has only brought me pain and I don't know, I can't see where it's leading. I had help and she was pulled right away. For the moment, the decision has been made for me."

Then Samuel went and sat on the bed. He took her hands in his. It was the first time he has ever touched her or stayed that close to her. "Samson is confused. I can tell you that for certain. He doesn't know what he is doing. If you leave this house Chika, I can guarantee you will never get him back. You will send him right in the direction he shouldn't go."

Chika looked at him. "What are you saying? What direction?"

He shook his head. "That is not important. Just don't go. Look for the answer. Search deep for solutions, but leaving isn't the solution because you will lose your daughter to us."

"You have never spoken to me like this before," she said.

He nodded. "I didn't know how to help you guys and I still don't know how. I did wish Samson never came back. But I understand you guys wouldn't have been able to get married without him coming back. Would your family have agreed?"

THE DELIVERANCE

She shook her head, trying to take in everything Samuel was saying.

He let go of her hands and got up. "Samson will be devastated to lose you. Look beyond what's going on right now to the man you married. He will be devastated. And if you decide to not leave anymore, I'm almost positive everything going on won't stop. But will you just hold on, please?"

"Thank you," Chika said.

"Belinda just found out she is pregnant," he surprised her. "But you cannot tell anybody, please. She's leaving tomorrow for the UK to start her Master's programme and her mum would go join her."

Chika congratulated him and watched him leave. She made up her mind to stay. For the time being.

When God pushes you to the edge, trust Him fully, because only two things can happen. Either He will catch you when you fall or He will teach you how to fly.

— unknown

Chapter Eighteen

Chika chose to stay for the time being. She listened to Samuel. But as he said, what was going on didn't go away. Samson didn't come any close to her. "If you want things to change, go and apologise." Chika knew she didn't do anything wrong. What would she be apologising for?

Temporarily without a maid, she couldn't go to work. Her friend, Iyanda, was mad when she heard what Titi did. "Three months? She stopped working for you three months ago? You must throw her out of your house."

"It is not my house," Chika said. She had opened up to Iyanda. All Stella employed Titi to do was to keep tabs on Chika in the house and report whether or not she went out with the baby. Titi was instructed not to assist Chika with the baby anymore because it wasn't her job.

One afternoon, while Sofia was napping, Chika quickly ran to the supermarket to get some items. Sofia had woken up crying and Titi didn't lift a finger to carry the baby.

"Titi will actually sit in the sitting room and watch me cleaning the house."

"Oh Chika, what will you do?"

She didn't know. She knew they had used Titi as a trap for her and Chika was determined not to fall into that trap. The girl kept pushing Chika's button, but every time, Chika forced herself to walk away.

Nikky had been so gracious with her. Opting to let her do her work from home since Chika had her equipment. But caring for Sofia and cleaning the house left her little time to make clothes. She missed important deadlines and finally told Nikky she couldn't.

"I'm sorry you are going through this," Nikky had said on the phone. "You are fighting a battle that isn't physical. It is spiritual and that's where you should take it."

Chika hadn't told Nikky anything about her life or what was going on in her home, but Nikky had picked up on it.

"Whenever you feel like working, even if it's one outfit you make for my store in a month, I will take it. A woman should always have a source of income, no matter how tiny and whether or not all your bills are being taken care of. I will be praying for you always. And know you can always count on me for anything."

THE DELIVERANCE

Chika had been touched by such generosity. When she got off the phone, she cried herself to sleep. That had been the week before.

"You have to fight on your knees," Iyanda said and brought Chika back into the present. Everyone who mattered in her life said the same thing to her. Fight on your knees. She had eventually told Ugochi everything, who in turn told her entire family.

What surprised Chika was the wave of support from all of them. They didn't scold her or remind her she was warned about the family she married into. Instead, they encouraged her to fight on her knees. Ugochi even gave a name to what Chika was experiencing: bewitchment.

"The day you feel you cannot take it anymore, or your life is threatened or there is no hope for your marriage, we are right behind you," her eldest sister, who had experienced some turbulence in her marriage in the past, told her.

Her mother started to call her every morning to pray with her. And because she turned down her family's offer to send her money since she didn't pay any bills in the house, her brother took it upon himself to ensure she always had airtime on her phone.

Her friend, Iyanda, also added Chika to a prayer group. "Things are already getting better, Chika. You too shall testify."

Chika was encouraged.

More and more, her heart yearned for peace. She didn't get married to live in an emotional war zone. She didn't get married to be a married single woman. She wanted everything that marriage gave. The warmth, love, companionship and a partner she could do life with. If apologising for a wrong that wasn't committed would give her those, she wasn't too proud to bend her knees. She did exactly what her husband had been requesting. When the whole family were together for Sunday lunch at Samuel, she went over and apologised. On her knees.

But it seemed as though a line had been drawn concerning her in the family and there was nothing she could do to cross it even after she apologised. It could be because she resumed making clothes in the house. She had a better routine with Sofia and was managing without pressure to meet deadlines on the clothes she made.

Maybe the Omoefes didn't like it that she had an alternative for income. Maybe that was what Stella meant the day Chika knelt before the whole family to say she was sorry for everything and causing so much trouble.

"You have to prove yourself, not only with words but with actions," Stella had said.

Chika knew she just couldn't stay not doing anything. Her hands had to be busy. She was determined never to ask Samson for money for anything. He always bought all their daughter's supplies without her asking but whenever there was something else Chika needed for the girl, she got it herself.

The only thing that changed after she apologised to his family was Samson who started sleeping at home again, though at the end of their Queen bed, both of them facing away from each other. He also started eating her meals. They were cordial to each other and he started to take an interest in Sofia who was growing so fast. For that alone, Chika was grateful because the girl needed her father.

Their conversation revolved only around the baby. He never asked about her life or how she was faring.

One day, he met her in the kitchen. "Did you know Belinda is pregnant?" he asked her.

Chika didn't turn to look at him. "Really?"

"According to Samuel, she is almost due to give birth. Can you imagine?" Then she looked at him. "See how united Belinda and Samuel are?" he asked her. "You cannot get between them. They know how to play their cards. They are a good team."

Chika didn't know what he meant. Was he implying they weren't a good team? Did he blame her for his family coming between them?

Two months later, Belinda gave birth to a son. Samuel, Stella and their mother all travelled to see her. Samuel had gone on ahead of them. Because Belinda was away and her mother-in-law had to travel too, Chika was asked to temporary be in charge of the dry-cleaning firm. Given the situation, she couldn't say no. She had worked there before, nothing had changed. She knew the process and was able to do what was asked of her.

Initially, her mother-in-law had suggested she could go to work with Sofia and Titi could assist her again, but Chika refused that option. She was never going to leave her daughter in the care of Titi who showed her true colours for a little extra money. Instead, Chika asked her mum to come over for the period her mother-in-law would be away. Chika noticed too that since she resumed going to the dry-cleaning firm, Titi started to clean the house.

Chika's commitment to the firm reduced the time she had to make clothes, but Chika knew it was temporary. She didn't want to rock the boat. She wanted peace and her mother was there to ensure by the time she returned to Enugu, Chika and her husband were doing better. Since her mother came, every morning, she called Chika and Samson over for morning devotion. Chika and Samson had never prayed together as a couple. Not even in the beginning when they were closer.

THE DELIVERANCE

One evening in the kitchen, Chika asked her mother, "What are you and Samson always talking about anyway." Chika noticed they sit together to watch TV and Samson laughs with her mother.

"Chika, he is your husband. He is my son-in-law. He's a good man but there is something broken between the both of you. I know you hurt because he hasn't shielded you the way you expected him to, but you have to love him. If you give the enemy a little opening, he will take it and make it very wide."

One evening, Chika was getting ready to close when Samson showed up at the office to take her out.

Chika had become conscious of her behaviour around him because he was neither here nor there. She didn't know what went on in his head. She didn't even know how to take her mother's advice to love someone who showed her no reactions.

"Can we do dinner?" he asked.

"I need to get home to Sofia," she said.

"Your mum has her, right," he reminded her. "Come on, babe."

Babe? He had dropped 'babe' and had been calling her by her name. Chika nodded and allowed him to take her out.

Their outing was like a first date or a blind date. They were both unsure of each other. It's been months since they tried to get into the other's personal space, months since they started living as roommates. But that night, Chika felt something come alive in her and realised how much she still loved Samson. He didn't talk about the past. He said they should enjoy the present and take it one day at a time.

A fire was rekindled. It turned out to be her best night in almost a year since she had Sofia. They took the fire home with them, both of them happy to discover the bliss they once had. Chika remembered their trip to celebrate their second anniversary. She was that happy again. She allowed herself to believe the troubles were behind them. The emotional war was over. She had her husband back. To ensure what has been reborn didn't die again, she considered working at the dry-cleaning firm when Samson's mum returned. She could work there only thrice a week. She knew she was dreaming. But Chika wanted peace. She wanted the new bliss to remain.

Sofia turned one while the others were still away and they celebrated with a few close friends whom they hadn't been in contact with for a while.

Her mother-in-law did not return from the UK. Stella returned alone after six weeks. Samuel took time away from work to be with his wife and son. Because Belinda's mother was in the UK, Mrs. Omoefe insisted on staying back to care for her grandson. Chika could only imagine what the situation would be like for Belinda. But she reminded herself Belinda was used to the woman. They worked together and Belinda knew how to be the Yes Ma girl that their mother-in-law favoured.

Chika wasn't bothered. For all she cared, the woman could remain in the UK forever. In her absence, when Stella returned, and because Chika's mum was still around, Stella moved back home to be with their father. Though they were cordial, Chika prayed Stella wouldn't return to the house.

When Chika discovered she was pregnant again, she and Samson were over the moon. She knew her mother was also very happy. This was the period her mother-in-law finally returned.

The enemy wins when you quit praying.

— www.lauraradniecki.com

Chapter Nineteen

After their mother returned, Stella moved back into the house the following day and Chika's newfound peace gradually took a back seat. She knew she was trapped. Going abroad to see Belinda was their opportunity of getting her to work at the firm. She didn't care. She had made up her mind to stay. When her mother-in-law asked her what her plans were, Chika told her she would work three days a week.

The woman was excited. "You have made the best decision of your life."

"There're just two problems, Mum. Can Titi move out of the house?" Chika requested. "And, my mother is going. I don't know what I will do about Sofia."

Her mother-in-law thought about it. "Sofia is more than one now and since you are busy, she can start creche. Have you found a good school where Sofia can go to creche?"

"No, Mum," she lied. Chika didn't bother. Her mother-in-law's friend owned a big school in Lekki and Samson had casually mentioned that Sofia will go there. She wouldn't oppose any decision that was good for her child.

"I will speak with Mrs. Ayoola then. Don't worry about my granddaughter. She will be well taken care of," the woman sighed. "As for Titi, I will think about it."

The next day, Stella fired Titi and asked her to leave the house. Chika didn't think she had to feel sorry for the stupid girl. Though she got one problem out, her troubles with her in-laws did not automatically go away. After a few weeks, her mother-in-law wanted her to work full-time.

"You know Belinda helped me a lot and she came every day. Since she left, there's been a vacuum here. Some positions should only be managed by us. You have to start coming in Mondays to Fridays.

Those two days were the days Chika did most of her sewing. She knew they wanted her to stop sewing completely, but she wasn't going to give up what was hers. Every day, either in the morning or at night, she invested two hours into making clothes. She also made good use of her Saturdays. Casual wear for children always sold off. Sofia as well as Iyanda's children were her models. She photographed them with one of Samson's cameras she learnt to use. Social media was her platform and she was happy to showcase the little she could do.

THE DELIVERANCE

"I am excited, Chika!" Nikky, her former boss, cooed. "I cannot wait to see your transformation. Congratulations my dear, but don't relax in your spiritual war room."

Daring to take the challenge, Chika employed two people who came on Saturdays to help her with her sewing.

Everything was going smoothly. Chika took her maternity leave from the dry-cleaning firm when she was eight months pregnant. Sewing wasn't very easy for her during that period but her two staff were great. From just working Saturdays, they became full-time and her business continued.

Chika pretended not to notice Stella's reaction whenever she came into the room they worked from and saw Chika cutting fabrics, or fixing buttons or other little details.

"So, you are still working," Stella would say.

"I'm only supervising," Chika explained.

"Okay o."

After Sylvester was born, her mother-in-law again wanted her to go to their house once she was discharged, but this time, Samson refused. Chika saw the look that crossed the woman's face and she knew they were about to go back ten thousand miles after she and Samson had taken one thousand miles forward.

A day after she got home with her baby, her mother-in-law came. "Chika, these people that are sewing clothes for you cannot continue coming into my house," her mother-in-law dropped. "There is a new baby in the house. It is not safe."

Chika hadn't finished digesting that when her mother-in-law dropped another one.

"Chika, I also need a room. Since you refuse to bring my grandson to the house, I am coming to stay to take care of him too."

There were four bedrooms in the house. Chika and Samson had the Master's bedroom. Stella had one. Sofia's nursery had been redone, to accommodate a bed for her mother and a toddler's bed for Sofia and the baby had the cot. The fourth room downstairs was where she worked.

"Oh, and I want a room upstairs so I can be more comfortable. Have the room ready in one week. After my grandson's naming ceremony, I am moving in here."

"That will be good my in-law," Chika's mother spoke up, "because I am leaving the day after the naming ceremony."

Chika's jaw dropped. But could she blame her mother?

"Oh my in-law, is that so?" Samson's mother returned. "Anyway, I am sure Chika is experienced enough now and can handle the baby on her own. With my help, of course."

Chika got the message. Her mother-in-law wanted Chika's mum to leave. There was no option of her bunking with Stella the permanent resident, or even staying next door with Samuel who had all four bedrooms to himself. Her mother-in-law, without saying so, also wanted to force Chika to stop sewing.

Chika cried in her room and begged her mother not to go. "What about his circumcision? How will I cope with Sofia?" Her mother had to stay two extra weeks.

They moved the cot and Sofia's bed into the Master's bedroom and Samson volunteered to sleep in the room downstairs after the sewing equipment were moved to the side and the bed Titi used was reset. Chika's mother stayed with her and the children.

Chika's two staff had already stopped coming since her mother-in-law's pronouncement. Chika told them it was temporary, pending when she found a solution to their workspace issue.

Her mother was sad to leave, but she couldn't stay. The environment was toxic and Samson's mum was very disrespectful. "My in-law, are you still around? I thought you said you were leaving," Samson's mum would say with a smile, or she would say, "My in-law, I am going to work. So that we can have enough money to eat and pay the bills in this house for your comfort."

"God will help you Chika. I am never going to stop praying for you but do your best. If I stay, we will end up fighting one day and you wouldn't want that. She will get tired and return to her husband. And you also need your husband to help you with the children."

And then her mother left.

"Chika," her mother-in-law would start. "Are you sleeping? Who is making my food? And my bathroom is dirty. When was the last time you cleaned this house?" She had wanted to take a new maid but her mother-in-law said no maid was coming into the house. "It is not like you have resumed work. What do you need a maid for?" The plan was to keep her so busy that even the little time she saw to release the tension through sewing, was taken away from her. Chika didn't know what she was being punished for again. She wasn't sleeping. She wasn't doing well.

One morning, while feeding Sofia, her mother-in-law came down. "Give me my breakfast," she said. Chika served her.

"Sylvester is three months old and can go to creche now. I have told Mrs. Ayoola to expect him, so you can come back to work."

"Okay, Mum."

"But you cannot bring people to make clothes in this house anymore," her mother-in-law added.

"Okay, Mum."

"And did Stella mention you have to start working on Saturdays too? More clients are beginning to prefer Saturday business and I want you to personally supervise the workers so they don't ruin our reputation."

"Okay, Mum."

The woman smiled. "So, when are you resuming?"

Chika shook her head. "I am sorry, Mum, I cannot come back to work now."

"Okay. When do you want to resume?"

Chika thought about it long and hard and made up her mind she wasn't going to compromise if they weren't willing to meet her halfway. "I am not." She didn't want to be a prisoner simply because she was seeking peace so they could all pretend around each other.

The woman was quiet. "Okay," she said eventually.

When Samson heard she decided not to return to the dry-cleaning firm, he was concerned. "Do you want to reconsider your decision?" she shook her head.

That week, she was told she couldn't bring Sofia to school because her fees hadn't been paid. She called Samson but he couldn't do anything. "This is all your fault," he exploded on the phone. "I don't have any access anymore to any money," he said and cut the call.

For a week, Samson did not come home. He stayed with his parents. His mother had conveniently moved back home.

God was extremely merciful and kind towards Chika. He sent people her way, who stood by her, gave her strength and showed her unconditional love. When her in-laws rained their torments, they didn't imagine she could endure it. The more they hindered her options, the more alternatives Chika had to move on.

Life pushed her out of her shell and showed her the new meaning of hustling because she wasn't going to let her parents or siblings shoulder her responsibilities.

She got a cheaper school for Sofia and put Sylvester in a creche. They used the school bus because Chika's car was taken away from her. During the hours they were away, Chika worked hard to ensure the children remained in school. The security had instructions not to allow anybody into the compound, so Chika never had visitors or help. If she wanted to see anyone, she went to meet them.

Samson returned home but moved his thing into the room his mother vacated. He was still angry because she didn't return to work for his mother. But he attended to the children when he was home.

THE DELIVERANCE

Chika held her head up and it infuriated those who wanted to be infuriated. She was past caring. As long as her life wasn't threatened, and her children were doing well, she could endure. And she did. Longer than she expected.

For we are not fighting against flesh-and-blood enemies, but against evil rulers and authorities of the unseen world, against mighty powers in this dark world, and against evil spirits in the heavenly places.

— Ephesians 6:12

Chapter Twenty

One Saturday afternoon, on their sixth anniversary, after carefully setting the table, Chika made for the bedroom to call Samson.

"Babe," she smiled at him. "The table is set for lunch." Behind her smile was fear of being rejected yet again. He didn't raise his head to look at her. More and more, his phone had replaced her position in his life. "Babe..." she started again.

"I heard you," he grunted. "I'm not hungry."

"Babe, can you at least ..."

"I said, I am not hungry!" he snapped as he got up. He paced up and down a little before storming past her.

She followed him carefully down the stairs. He paused and looked at the dining table, then turned to speak to her.

"I'm going to watch football."

Seconds later, she heard the key turn in the lock and he was gone. Again.

Sing. Sing. Sing.

She heard in her spirit, sing. She didn't feel like singing. She was getting tired. Had God abandoned her? Didn't she have the conviction about the man that she married? How long was she going to cry? It was their sixth wedding anniversary. She knew they had nothing to celebrate. She was only hoping that they could pretend to be happy and in love for that day. And just maybe, they could enjoy the pretence and something would snap in his head and turn him back into the man she fell in love with.

Her wishes shattered right before her.

She turned to look up and saw Stella's head sticking out. Their eyes met and Stella retreated. But her message was succinctly passed. She wanted Chika to know she witnessed her humiliation yet again. Behind the door, she would call her mother to share the good news of Chika's planned sixth wedding anniversary celebration and how her brother walked out on her.

Sing.

No. she didn't want to sing. At that point, she doubted what she was hearing anyway. It felt like God led her to the wilderness and forgot to lead her through it.

THE DELIVERANCE

Then she laughed and approached the dining table. She worked overtime to meet a client's job just so she could get paid to organise the special lunch that was rejected.

Iyanda even took the kids off her so she could have alone time with her husband. They fasted and prayed about that day to be the beginning of a new chapter in Chika's marriage.

Stella wasn't meant to be in the house. She knew Stella had a wedding to attend out of town that weekend because she bought the Asoebi, paraded it in front of Chika and called a fashion designer to come to the house to take her measurement, just to spite Chika.

Stella was meant to leave the day before but didn't. Maybe she remembered it was her brother's anniversary and didn't want to leave Chika and her brother alone in the house. Maybe her mother advised her to stay put for the same reasons.

As far as they were concerned, Chika must never be happy or enjoy her marriage. They liked where Chika was. Alone and struggling with the children. Ignored by her husband.

"Satan!" Chika called out. "You are a liar!" she spat as she pulled out a chair and sat down. Had Samson not walked out, he would have been sitting at the head of the table, just beside her.

She allowed her eyes to rest on the empty chair and imagined him sitting there.

"The man I married is patient and kind," she said to the chair. "He is not boastful or proud or rude. The Samson that I married is not irritable. He keeps no record of my wrongs. The man I married hates injustices and upholds the truth. He never gives up. He never loses faith. He is always hopeful and endures through every circumstance.

"And this is also the woman you married. Our love will last forever. Whoever opposes us will have to go a different path from us because God will give us peace. We will have peace."

Sing.

She heard in her spirit again. And as she opened her mouth to sing, she heard Stella coming down the stairs and then towards the dining table. Stella stopped to look at everything Chika did.

"Hmm," she started. "My brother did not even stay to celebrate your happy wedding anniversary. Na wa o!" she was being sarcastic. "And you even tried o. See all the things you did. If you had involved me, we should have invited the whole family and Samson definitely, wouldn't leave the house when he's supposed to be celebrating. But you wanted to do 'me and my husband'. Anyway, happy anniversary," she smiled at Chika. It was a smile of victory.

At that moment, a song exploded in Chika's spirit. Jehovah has the final say. And the message of the song poured a smile out of her. "Thank you," she said as she pushed her chair back and got to her feet.

Chika carefully rearranged the table so Stella got the message not to touch anything. Samson would return home and they would celebrate.

But Samson did not return. He went to his parents' place for a few days. Chika praised through it. She believed the words of knowledge she has been given. Her deliverance was on the way.

Behold, God is my salvation; I will trust, and will not be afraid; for the Lord God is my strength and my song and he has become my salvation.

— Isaiah 12:2

Chapter Twenty-One

One July afternoon, a week after Sylvester's third birthday and a few days to Sofia's fifth, Samson knocked on the door and entered. Chika stopped what she was doing at the sewing machine.

"I noticed the kids aren't home," he said.

Chika told him they were at Iyanda's place. "I will pick them up later in the evening.

Samson nodded. "How are they doing at school?"

"Good."

"Chika, I just came to apologise," he started. "I know they are my responsibility. As soon as I can, I promise to take it over and refund you."

Chika shook her head. "That won't be necessary. They are my children too."

He nodded. He looked like he wanted to say something else and she waited. "Are you happy?" he asked finally.

She smiled and thought of how to answer. "I am not sad," she said instead and it was true. She was in a better place.

"Chika," he started again. "I came to ask if I can come back to our bedroom and the kids go to theirs."

She wanted to remind him he left more than 2 years earlier, on his own. But she bit her lips. "Samson, this is not my house. If you even want me to leave the bedroom for you, I can."

He shook his head. "I want us to try to work things out. I am tired, Chika."

Chika looked at him and remembered Iyanda's favourite phrase to her. "You too shall testify." Was this the beginning of her testimony? Chika had been in a spiritual battle for a long time. On four different occasions, she made up her mind to leave the house but ended up not leaving. She couldn't leave her children and she couldn't give up on Samson. She believed in what they had. She believed he was the one for her. In a way, she felt responsible for leading him back home. She couldn't leave him in the same entanglement he once ran away from.

"When you look at your husband, who do your see?" one of her mentors asked her one time she said she couldn't take it anymore. "Is he happy?"

"No."

THE DELIVERANCE

"Do you think your husband is intentionally acting the way he is with you?"

"No."

"What do you want, Chika?"

"I want my husband back. I want my marriage to work. I want us to be happy with our children."

"Then don't give up. Deliverance will come," she had been advised.

As she looked at her husband, she wondered if this was the deliverance she and her circle of influence and praying partners had been waiting for. But there was something she wanted to clarify.

"Can you sit down? Let's talk. Okay," she started. "I am willing to try to work things out," she said.

"It's just that I don't have any money right now, Chika."

She frowned. "Do we need money to work things out?"

Samson released a deep breath. "I want us to leave this house. Take what's ours and go start our lives."

Her hand flew to cover her mouth. She couldn't believe it. And it occurred to her she never considered that option before. She always thought she had to be the only one to leave and leave the kids behind. Of course, they could leave together with their children. And as she looked at him, she realised that decision had to come from him.

"I look at you, Chika. I see how well you have managed around the challenges and it suddenly dawned on me, that we actually can," his eyes teared up. "I'm sorry, babe. I'm sorry it took me this long to see it."

Later, when Chika began to draw from her experience to encourage others who were going through challenges, she told them that many times, people do not recognise the beginning of deliverance.

"Because life goes through a process and God made it that way, sometimes, our deliverance isn't sudden," Chika would say. "Not because God cannot change situations suddenly, but because of the benefits of the process."

Her deliverance started long before she realised it. Her deliverance was in play when she bought her equipment and it didn't seem like she would use them. It was in play when sewing was all she could turn to, to maintain her sanity and release the tension. It was in play when she could work to keep the children in school.

God used her struggles to show Samson that they would be fine without the family's money. Samson had been afraid since Sofia was born that he wouldn't be able to provide for his family. He wanted them to be comfortable. He gave up pursuing his dreams so the children could be fine. The devil kept reminding him how difficult it was for him to get a job the first time he left the family and his friend Maro had to support him.

Chika's heart poured praises to God. The past years of dedicating her life to her work and the children, the sacrifices she made to acquire more knowledge along the way, and the trainings and counselling she had been involved in, were all God's plans towards getting her to where she needed to be.

Chika got a bus to help her move her sewing equipment.

"Ha, have you gotten a shop? Or are you moving out?" Stella asked.

"I won't be sewing from here anymore," Chika said.

"Thank God," Stella said before leaving.

Chika and Samson agreed not to let anyone know their plans. Before approaching Chika that day, Samson had spoken with Nikky. He met her for lunch and told her everything she didn't know. She was the first person to know about his plans.

"But I don't have the money to get a place. I am embarrassed by the idea of even asking Chika after all she has been through. That is if she is even willing to go with me." Nikky encouraged him to talk to Chika and offered her support in whatever ways they needed.

When Chika and Samson decided, Nikky made Chika a partnership offer she'd been nursing. And the money from it was more than enough to get a comfortable place.

Chapter Twenty-Two

Before they eventually left, Samson invited the family over. He wasn't going to leave the way he did the other time. Chika was apprehensive about it, but she decided to trust God on the final lap of their deliverance.

Samson thanked his parents for their love. "But it's time for me to go with my family," he said.

Chika could feel Stella and her mother-in-law looking at her. But she looked straight ahead.

"The same way you built a legacy for yourself, I am going to build one for myself," Samson continued.

"So, you are abandoning us again," his mother said.

"No, Mum. I will always be around. I'm your son."

"Where will you go?" Samuel asked. He had a twinkle in his eyes. "How will you get by?"

Samson smiled at him and Chika realised they must have discussed it. "I will find something to do."

"He is going to take pictures," Stella said. "And this silly girl here must have used a charm on him again."

"Enough," their father finally found his voice. He looked at Chika for a while. He was going to say something to her but changed his mind. "Stella, get on the laptop now and transfer Samson's salary to him. All the backlog. From the time he started working at Safe Travels."

"But Dad…" she started.

"Do it!"

"No!" his wife countered. "He's been living in my house without paying rent. He's been spending money from the company's accounts."

"I don't want anything," Samson said. "I just want to go. Come on, babe."

"Sit down!" his father commanded. "Okay. Stella. I know you. You have a record of every single withdrawal or transaction Samson made. Right?"

"Yes," Stella agreed grudgingly.

"Good. As the accountant that you are, calculate his backlog right now and deduct the total of that record you have," Mr. Omoefe said.

"He lived for free in my house. He and his wife used my cars," his wife told him.

THE DELIVERANCE

Mr. Omoefe smiled. "I am not done. How long did Chika work at the dry-cleaning firm? Stella, you also have her backlog salary. She was in a management position, mind you. But you can keep it. That will cover the rent of the cars they used even if you withdrew Chika's car years back.

"Now, the house rent for the seven years they've been here, divide it into two, deduct it from Samson's backlog and give him whatever balance is left. I want to see it."

His wife flared up. "Why should Samson only pay half the rent?"

"Because Stella lives here too," her husband reminded her. "Samson pays half, only."

The drama that unfolded that day had been messy. Mrs. Omoefe owned everything. It wasn't her husband. It was all her money, her businesses, her properties. She had bossed him around for years. She held the children in a tight grip. She controlled the family and her words were lord until that day.

The only child who knew the truth was Stella. She was her mother's PA in everything.

They've been in their new place for more than six months. They were happy. They were on a journey of discovery and vigorously pursuing their dreams. They had a great support system around them. Samson was also back in the loop with his friends and department members from church.

When deliverance came for Chika, it extended beyond her immediate family. She went through those challenges for Samuel, Solomon and their father to be delivered as well. God used her pain to bring freedom to others.

The nature of the enemy's warfare in your life is to cause you to become discouraged and to cast away your confidence. Not that you would necessarily discard your salvation, but you could give up your hope of God's deliverance. The enemy wants to numb you into a coping kind of Christianity that has given up hope of seeing God's resurrection power.

— Bob Sorge

Acknowledgements

To the many gifts of men from God to me. Men turned brothers and women turned sisters; a family that has brought such richness to my life.

I love you forever and ever.

To the team of photographers I get to do business life with, partners who allow me to hold them accountable unashamedly.

Thank you for standing with me.

I couldn't have asked God for more loyal and true friends to journey with me in this life.

To my many Mentors, Coaches, head correctors, and people who call me out on my bullshits.

Thank you for your diligence to polish this girl.

I'm in awe of God and His creations.

Thank you Uzezi for editing this book; Onyi for a beautiful cover design and Segun for the creative cover artwork.

I am grateful to my family—my husband, Oluwafemi; daughter, Susan the first and son, Royalty like no other. My parents, Mr and Mrs Ojo; my siblings OlaDele, OluwaBukola, OluwaToyin and Olamilekan, I'm also grateful. In one way or the other, you've all contributed to my becoming.

To God, the Father, our Lord Jesus Christ and the Holy Spirit, Thank You for saving me completely from my sins, for adopting me as Your daughter (I can be a handful) — it's priceless!

Manufactured by Amazon.ca
Bolton, ON